The Tin Church

Rosamund Haden

The Tin Church

Rosamund Haden

First published in 2004 in Southern Africa by
David Philip Publishers, an imprint of New Africa Books (Pty) Ltd,
99 Garfield Road, Claremont 7700, South Africa

ISBN 0-86486-635-6

Cover photo © Lien Botha
Design and typesetting by Charlene Bate
Printed and bound by CTP Book Printers,
Duminy Street, Parow, Cape Town, South Africa

For my family

There is laughter
and footprints in the red dust that has settled on the floorboards in the tin church
The sound of two pairs of feet running
Two summer dresses.

Prologue: 1990

A child found the bones. She was on her way from her father's kraal to buy sugar from the store at Hebron. The storm broke as she reached the path that wound up through the koppies to the tin church that stood on the ridge, overlooking the farms. The clouds split open and heavy drops of rain pelted the ground as she scrambled up the granite boulders and between the euphorbias that stood like sentinels. She crouched under a cabbage tree for shelter but the leaves brushed against her skin and soon she was soaked and had to push her way further in between the rocks. There was an opening like a tunnel between two boulders. It was narrow, but she pushed her way through and found herself on a flat piece of ground. Below her the valley stretched as far as the mountain ridge that marked the end of the highveld and the descent into Swaziland and down into the lowveld.

She crouched down, leaning against the rocks, and it was here, in the red earth that had turned to mud, that she found the bones. She had seen the skulls of animals: baboons, cattle, sheep, even dogs lying bleached by the sun in the veld, but she recognised that this was different.

The skull was tilted back, staring at her. The water ran in through the eyes and the jaws that were upturned towards the sky as though it was drinking the rain. Somebody had dug it up along with other bones that must have belonged to arms and legs; there were long slash marks in the soil.

She turned and ran, scratching her legs on the thorn bushes, until she reached the church. Here she sat shivering until the drumming of her heart slowed down and then she took off again, sliding in the mud down the slope, past the river pool and along the path to the farm school.

A boy was running up and down the stoep of the school, putting down enamel basins to catch the water that poured through the leaking roof. '*Ufunani*?' he asked the girl, but she didn't answer and he went back into the classroom to get help. When the schoolteacher came out he found the girl next to the door, shaking.

★

It only stopped raining the next day and by then the bones had gone. Somebody had taken them from the burial site.

★

After the storm, in the dusk, a warm gust of wind blew over the veld, up the road past the school and the store and down the avenue of gum trees that led to the house at Hebron. It carried the news of the human bones that the girl had found. Gathering speed, it blew up the flight of stone steps and under the huge arched wooden door that had been brought all the way from Holland. It shot over the expanse of carpet and wove between the legs of the grand piano and blew through the door on the far side of the room that led into the inner courtyard around which the house was built. Here it circled the roses and the prickly pear tree and made a lizard run for cover.

Catherine King was sitting in front of the window in her bedroom that led off the courtyard. She held a baby bird that she had rescued from the storm in her old paper-thin hands. The rain had washed it out of its nest on the roof and she had found it struggling to lift itself from a puddle in the courtyard. She had mashed together some bread and milk and chewed it until it was soft. Now she held the bird up so that it could peck the food out of her mouth. When it had fed, she put it in the cardboard box and looked for a piece of newspaper she could tear up to keep the bird warm. She found a yellowed sheet in the cupboard and was about to tear it up when she stopped. It was dated June 1970 – the year the police had come and arrested the black schoolteacher – they had taken him away and he hadn't come back. She had tried to stop the police from searching the church but they had turned over the pews and gone through the hymn books looking for illegal pamphlets. The workers had come up to the house in the middle of the night to escape the police searches.

Now it was the farmers who were frightened – something had started that they couldn't stop. She had overheard them talking at the shops in town – they were letting black leaders out of prison; there would be a terrible blood bath; they would ruin the country.

Catherine started to tear the paper into thin strips to line the box. It had been twenty years since this paper had wrapped something from the shops. It had been twenty years since there had been three of them living in the house at Hebron: Maria, Tom and her.

The wind blew the door open and one of the windows came unlatched and banged against its frame. She went to close it before the glass shattered. As she fixed the latch, she looked up to the ridge between the farms and saw a light burning inside the church.

Maria Dlamini stood in the kitchen doorway at Hebron. She could see the strip of light under Catherine's door across the courtyard. She turned back inside the kitchen and looked at the clock on the wall; it was upside down. Standing on a chair, she turned it the right way round, wondering how long it had been that way and why she hadn't noticed. It had stopped anyway, but it didn't matter, as she knew the time by the darkness of the sky. It was time to feed the animals. They came first, Catherine told her – she didn't agree, but she went on feeding them. She took five old metal dishes from the shelf and arranged them in a line in the courtyard. Then she took a large urn and poured milk out into the dishes. She called out into the dark. The cats came out of the shadows; their forms slunk along the walls. They swiped at each other, their eyes infected and leaking pus. Maria watched them as they wove around the dishes; she kicked at the ones that were fighting, to separate them.

Catherine came out of her room and crossed the courtyard. Maria couldn't see her face but she knew something was wrong from the way Catherine hunched her shoulders. When she had disappeared inside, Maria went into the kitchen and took the chicken and vegetables out of the oven and carried them across to the sitting room. She found Catherine sitting at the table; she looked pale and her fingers played with the frayed edge of the tablecloth. If Maria spoke now Catherine would snap at her.

Maria couldn't remember when she had started eating with Catherine. Sometimes she and Catherine would eat in the kitchen together with Gabriel who worked in the garden. It was practical, Catherine had explained. There was less time wasted in cooking and washing up – Gabriel had to eat after all or he would stop working so hard.

Maria had told her how the workers were striking in the cities. Gabriel's son had bought a gun. The movement for freedom was like a river in full flood now – there was no stopping it. They must get on a boat and ride with it or they would drown.

She could say these things to Catherine. She had known her for seventy years. They were born in the same year and the same month on the farm, Hebron.

They ate in silence and before Catherine had finished she pushed her plate away and stood up.

'I'm going to bed.' She walked over to fetch the paraffin lamp from the shelf.

'One of the children at the school found a human skull and bones below the church. When they went back to look they were gone.' Maria watched Catherine's face to see what effect her words would have, but Catherine didn't respond; she just picked up the lamp and turned to leave the room. When she did speak, she didn't look at Maria.

'Put some more wood in the stove, I don't want cold water.' She closed the door behind her.

In her room she sat down in front of the mirror. White hair, blue eyes, one clouded by a cataract now. Her hair was soft. She would cut some to line the bird's nest. She ran her finger over the scar on her left cheek, where she had fallen from her horse into a thorn bush.

She wondered who had dug up the bones after all these years, and why.

*

Maria stacked the plates and took them through to the kitchen. She picked at the chicken carcass and washed the bits down with some cheap red wine Gabriel had left her. Then she went to her room next to the kitchen. There was nothing left to do but sleep. Her steel bed was up on bricks, not because of the tokoloshe but because of the river that came at night now. It brought visions of things in the past – of people she had lost on dark nights when the police came or those who had crossed borders to escape. It brought things in the future. She saw leaders with black stripes painted across their faces on illegal posters on city walls – the stripes were being torn off and she could see their eyes now; staring out at her; they were coming back.

She saw Catherine and herself as young girls running down the dusty road to the store and looking up at the church as it shone in the dark. She saw the bones.

It was still dark when she woke up. Her mouth was dry. She pulled the grey blanket around her shoulders and went out into the courtyard. The sky had cleared and the moon was full. It was lovely, but she couldn't stop and look too long – she was worried. The slates were cold under her bare feet as she crossed the courtyard. Catherine's door was open – she was gone.

Part One

Catherine

Catherine had taken a torch with her when she left the house and packed a bag with a blanket and water. She wouldn't need the torch outside, as the moon was full and she could have found her way along the path with her eyes shut. She wasn't afraid of being killed in the dark – not like the women she had overheard in town talking of murder on the farms. Catherine took the torch because the light might go out in the church and she wanted to see what had been left there for her – because she knew he had left something even if he hadn't waited for her to get there.

The path led down alongside the dirt road, between the gum trees to the farm school where it bent away from the road, winding around the base of the koppies and down towards the river. Here it split into two. One branch led up the slope to the tin church. The other continued straight down to the water. She took the branch that led down to her river, and her pool. There was a breeze blowing up off the water. It rustled the reeds on the banks of the river. She had taken off her shoes and felt the earth under her feet. The path was narrow and the grasses, silver in the moonlight, brushed her legs as she walked. She remembered running down this path with Maria and laughing as they dived into the water. But now the body that carried her was thin and brittle with age and it was her mind that ran ahead of her, uncontained in the dark. When she reached the water she spread her blanket out and sat down to rest. The river curved, forming a pool. On the far side the rocks rose steeply out of the water and at the top there was a clump of wattle trees. Behind these stood the church.

The pool was full from the summer rains. Down below it the river widened and curved through the land, fat and heavy as a python. Catherine knew every part of it that ran through the farm. She had swum, canoed and walked its length. In the dry winters when the highveld grasses turned yellow, the river would be shallow and stagnant. In the summer it swelled with the rain and the banks baked under the sun and the grass was lush and green and dotted with pink and white cosmos flowers and wild mushrooms. She had swum here in thunderstorms, watching the lightning strike the tops of the iron rocks on the hills behind the farm.

Now when she looked up from the river pool she could see the light still burning in the church through the branches of the trees. There was a whisper in the wind, a warm breath: her father's voice.

⋆ ⋆ ⋆

'Can you see the rabbit in the moon, Katie?'

'Yes, I see it. And I can see the Southern Cross.'

'Clever girl.'

I am eight and I am clever. I was born on 20 January 1923. That is History – we had to write it for schoolwork. I live on our farm called Hebron. It is three hours in the car North East of Johannesburg – that is Geography. I have never been to Johannesburg, I have never been off the farm but I can read long books and I know about a lot of things like the stars and how to kill chickens. 'Look at the moon in the water,' Dad says.

I take a stone and throw it into the centre of the shining ball and watch the ripples.

'It's late.' Dad swings me up onto his shoulders. I put my hands on his head. He runs up the path away from the pool, out onto the dust road that leads up to the house. The gum trees are high over our heads; the leaves are dancing against the sky. I shriek and cling on to Dad's head. He slows down when he gets to the posts at the beginning of our driveway. A truck rattles past; I see the headlights and the dust clouds around us, we are covered in dust and it makes us cough.

Dad makes me laugh. He changes things – like when you switch on a light in a room and you can see things suddenly, all bright and shining in different colours.

There is a light on in the sitting room. No other lights are on in the house. We are the only ones awake. The boards in the passage creak under Dad's boots. He swings me down onto my bed and tells me it's time to sleep and promises he will take me down the river on the raft he built and he'll take me down the krantz where the leopard lives. My sister, Lilly, stirs in her sleep but she doesn't wake up. She makes small whistling sounds. I can see her eyes moving under her eyelids. She is the baby; my games are too rough for her. She's too young to join in and she runs and hides behind Mum's skirts for protection and tells Mum that I pinched her and Mum slaps me.

Dad is fishing in his pockets for something. He takes out a seedpod that rattles and puts it under Lilly's pillow so she'll find it in the morning. He has something for me too. He is always taking things out of his pockets: a compass so that I can map the veld, a bird on a spring that winds up and flies, marbles of all colours, African trade beads – I keep them all in a box under my bed. Tonight it is a parcel in brown wrapping paper. I tear at it, impatient to see inside.

It's a photograph in a silver frame; the one Mum took at the river. She used to take a lot of photographs; she even changed a room in the back of the house into a darkroom where she developed the prints. She didn't take ordinary pictures though – the ones you see in family albums. She took pictures of rocks and beetles and animals' skulls that she found in the veld. Sometimes you couldn't tell what the pictures were of – only she knew. She doesn't take photographs anymore; she stopped when Lilly was born. This is the last photograph she took.

It's at the river. I remember Dad teasing her, kissing her as they stood in the water. Then he picked me up and walked into the middle where the rocks made white water and he sat down with me on his knee.

He is wearing khaki shorts and a white shirt in the photograph. His hair is wet, so is mine. I am smiling – you can see the gap between my teeth. My face is dirty with mud from the river bank. I am wearing a tunic with peacocks embroidered along the neck.

There are peacocks behind the house, up the path where Maria lives. Maria Lindiwe Dlamini. Lindiwe means that she was waited for. She has a black name and a white one. I only have a white one – Catherine – but they call me Katie. Maria is eight too. Eight is a good number. If you put it on its side it goes on forever.

Maria's mum is our kitchen girl but she works in the whole house and she isn't a girl. We are girls. She is an adult. Sometimes Maria feeds the peacocks, but she says they frighten her at night because they sound like babies who have lost their mothers in the dark. They are crying, she says.

My legs are dark from the sun and my feet are bare in the picture. My arms are wrapped around Dad's neck. He is sitting on a rock in the river and the water is pouring over us. Our clothes are soaked but the sun is shining above our heads.

I remember Mum making us smile. 'Say cheese,' she said.

'Why cheese?' I asked.

'Why is everything a question with you?' she asked me, but she was laughing. We smiled and she pressed the button.

'For me?' I ask Dad but I know it is. I run my finger over the picture frame, it's old. There are patterns in the silver. I sleep with the photograph under my pillow so that I can dream about the water and the sunshine; it will spread through the pillow into my brain. When I wake up I am holding the photograph.

The early morning cold blue light is filling the room. I climb out of the window and jump down into the yard. Maria is waiting for me by the gate. She has her enamel mug. Hers is blue and mine is red.

We run up to the koppies together. We have a house there in the rocks where we play plummy ladies. We set down our mugs and collect leaves and stones. 'Would you like another cup of tea – with sugar and milk?' I have taught Maria to speak English. You should see people's faces when we go to town and she speaks it. She has taught me words in her language – it is Swazi. That is Languages.

I set out our table on the boulder. Two enamel mugs, twigs for spoons, stones for sugar lumps and the leaves are our plates. Then we invite the lizards to join us. There are two of them that have climbed up the rock face. They hold their bodies stiffly and lift their feet off the rock, one then the other, as if they were standing on a hot plate.

'Would you like sugar with your tea?' we ask them. They bob their heads up and down 'Yes,' they say, 'yes, we would like sugar with our tea.'

We get tired of playing in the rocks and go further up the slope to the tin church.

The door is open. We have been before; it's a good place to play. Maria is running ahead of me, she stops at the door and turns to me.

'Do you hear?'

I run up beside her and stop.

'What?' We stand and listen. A lady is singing in the church. I know the words, so does Maria, they are sad words for crying.

'Come.' Maria takes my hand, but I pull her back.

'We can't go inside.'

'Why?'

But I can't tell her why, I just know. We struggle in the dirt: when Maria pulls away from me the singing has stopped. When we get inside the church there is no one there.

* * *

Catherine moved her legs, her bones felt stiff. She wrapped the blanket closer around her shoulders and looked up at the trees above the pool. In those trees she and Maria had made a tree house and had broken off branches to sweep the floor of the church. Underneath the canopy of leaves they had taken off their clothes and painted themselves with mud.

* * *

'What were you doing up at the church, Catherine? You're covered in mud.' Mum calls me Catherine when she's angry. She takes the scrubbing brush to my skin to take the mud off. She looks tired. 'You knew we were going out to dinner. What did you think you were doing?'

I can't tell her, I can't tell anyone. It's our secret. I can hear Maria's screams. Her mum is beating her with a switch in the yard. The scrubbing brush is not so bad. I am squeezed into a dress I have outgrown, and bundled into the car with Lilly. Dad comes out of the house. He has shaved and put on his best shirt. He picks a white cosmos flower and spins it round in his fingers as he crosses the driveway. When he gets to the car he reaches in and puts it in my hair.

'Can Maria come?' I ask.

'No.'

'Why not?'

No answer.

'Why not?' I try again, louder this time.

'Will you stop!' Mum turns round and silences me with her eyes. Then she turns back and stares straight out in front of her. Her face is still, like she's gone away somewhere, like she's not there.

Lilly sticks her tongue out at me and I pinch her to make her scream. I wind down the window and lean out to wave at Maria as we pass. She is sitting on the gate at the entrance to the driveway sucking a skinned prickly pear. I can see the blood on her legs where the stick cut her skin.

We arrive at the Coombes' house and stand waiting in the dark hallway. The big grandfather clock is ticking. Mrs Coombe comes towards us. Her long skirt rustles like leaves when you rake them. Lilly pinches me to get me back for the car. Mum's hand slaps at us behind her back while she's smiling at Mrs Coombe. Her face is all stretched. Dad bends his head and kisses Mrs Coombe's hand. He looks at her and I feel something. I don't know what it is, but it's like electricity – it makes the room uneasy. 'Don't stare,' Mum whispers, and puts her warning hand on my shoulder. I shake it off.

We go through to the dining room. The servant stands in the corner of the room like a statue. Mrs Coombe's skin is cool and china-smooth, like the shell of an egg. We say grace before we eat. Next time we come to dinner I will bring a teaspoon, and tap it against her skin to see what sound it makes.

Mrs Coombe reaches over and lifts the lid off the dish that is waiting in the middle of the table. I laugh out loud in terror and then cover my mouth as Mum frowns at me. I look at Dad for help. Then I look back at what sits there on the china. The huge red tongue has been pulled out by the roots. You can see the fine hairs on the skin.

'Carve, darling, why don't you?' Mrs Coombe hands Mr Coombe the silver knife. She lifts her top lip and I see where she has got lipstick on her teeth in a pink stain.

Mr Coombe smiles across the table at Mum. With his wet fleshy lips he's like a toad. When he reaches for Mum's plate he tries to touch her fingers, and Mrs Coombe tinkles her dinner bell again. 'More potatoes, more beans, darling?' her voice is high.

Mr Coombe slides the tongue onto my plate. I cover it with potatoes so that I can't see it.

'What are you doing?' Lilly hisses. The tongue isn't there now. There is nothing but more potato under my potato. I kick her under the table. She is eating her tongue; she is going to finish soon – such a good little girl.

Then the Coombes' dog comes in and rubs its head against my leg under the table. I keep my eyes on Mrs Coombe's face as I slide the plate under the table and tip it up. The tongue slides into the dog's jaws. Snap, it's gone. It's all over. But Mrs Coombe has eyes that see everywhere. She was born like that.

Slowly she cuts another slice and puts it down on my plate. 'There,' she says and smiles. 'You don't want to miss out on a nice slice of tongue, do you?'

Lilly is allowed to go with the grown-ups through to the sitting room. I am left forever to finish the tongue. I sit alone in the dark dining room. Then Mrs Coombe's servant comes out from the shadows in the corner. He comes closer. If I were Lilly, I would scream right now, but I want him to come close. I want to feel his skin. It looks warm. He reaches for my plate. I watch while he takes the tongue, opens his mouth wide, and slides it down his throat. Then he puts the plate back down in front of me, just in time. Mrs Coombe comes through from the living room. 'Finished, have you?' She looks at my plate, and I nod.

Tomorrow I will come back and find out things about Mrs Coombe. I'll find out why she makes the air in the room feel funny like electricity. I'll find out why her skin looks so like an egg. I'll bring my teaspoon and tap it against Mrs Coombe and watch all her yellow yolk run out. Mum once turned over her hard-boiled egg after she had eaten it and drew a face on the shell. I asked her if it was Mrs Coombe and she said no, but it looked just like her, with thin pink lips and pencil eyebrows. Then she hit the egg over the head until it smashed. 'Oh dear,' she said, 'an accident,' and we laughed.

When we get home Mum sits on the edge of my bed and reads to us while Dad goes down the avenue to check that he has locked the store up. Mum reads out of a fairy-tale book from England. The pages are covered with fishmoth stains. The fishmoths have eaten away Blue Beard's beard. Fish moths, moth fishes, swimming under water, coming up to breathe and eat Sleeping Beauty's toes.

She looks up from the book and stares out of the window into the dark. Then she stands up and pushes the sleeves of her dress up as if she is going to wash her hands. She raises the wooden window frame. Lilly screams; she is afraid the bats will fly in.

'Can you hear that?' she turns to us, her face is tired.

'What?'

'Your Dad's coming. I'm sure I can hear him.' She has thin lips. When she bends to kiss me I can smell the rose scent on her.

'What? I can't hear anything.'

She switches off the light.

* * *

Catherine put her feet in the pool and spread her toes under the cool, dark water. Maria would have woken up by now, she thought. She always woke up in the middle of the night. Sometimes Catherine would hear her walking up and down the passages. The older she got the less she could sleep. There had been years when Maria hadn't slept at Hebron, but up at the church or at her mother's kraal. Now Catherine needed her in the house – there was no one else there if one of the animals got sick in the night and she needed to drive into town. More than once Catherine had woken up to find Maria standing over her bed watching her sleeping – checking that she was still breathing. It drove Catherine mad. But tonight Maria would find Catherine's bed empty and she would come out to look for her.

It was a climb up to the church. The last time Catherine had been up there was when one of her dogs had disappeared. She had found it with its leg caught in a trap and had taken off her shirt to bandage the wound, and then carried the dog up to the church. Sitting on the floor with the dog's head in her lap and its blood soaking her trousers, she had cried. It had come out like a cracked sob, as if she had forgotten how to cry; it had been so long. Then she had felt something that she hadn't for a long time – a brush against her skin, a sigh and her troubled mood had passed. When she had stood up she had found the strength to carry the dog back down the hill to Hebron.

Now, as she sat in the dark with her eyes closed, Catherine saw the shapes and colours of scenes that had been buried, emerging like images on her mother's photographic paper. She saw herself eating mangoes in the heat of summer – the yellow fruit staining her skin and making her fingers sticky. She saw herself diving into the pool and opening her eyes underwater – her skin was white, blue, brown, as she secretly lived out the excitement of a quiet life, emerging out of the water to dry like lichen on the rocks. She saw widow birds flying low over the water, dragging their heavy tails, and a snake drinking from the pool. And if she looked up she saw the wattle branches move above the pool and the shadow of someone watching her.

She could smell the earth and the sweat of cattle that moved in the darkness nearby and she put her head against the ground. Very faintly she felt a vibration on the path. Two sets of feet, running, far off, but coming closer.

* * *

'Hurry up, Katie.'

Maria is ahead of me on the path. We have been swimming in the river. We aren't allowed, but we do it anyway. Dad taught me but Mum says we are still too young to swim without adult supervision. But we are eight, which is old enough to do anything. Maria nearly drowned the other day. I had to rescue her. It gave us a fright.

'*Maye ba bo*,' she said, just like her gogo does. We rolled around in the grass all wet and laughing. When we were dry Maria plaited my hair. Her fingers are fast and they click like needles. My hair is wet now; Mum will know where we've been – there's no time to dry it in the sun because she is calling us in to lunch. I can hear her calling my name.

I catch up with Maria and pull at her skirt. 'Maria, guess what?'

'What?'

'I'm going to ride over to Mrs Coombe's after lunch. I'm going to find out what her secrets are. Will you come?'

'I can't, I got to clean at our place.'

'I'm going anyway.'

We run up the steps and into the kitchen. Mum is sitting at the table with Lilly, waiting.

'Where have you been?' She looks furious. She hardly ever smiles these days. I want to make her laugh again. She dishes the food out for us. As we wait for Dad to come home she keeps looking up at the clock on the wall. Lilly starts to whine because she's hungry. It makes Mum tense.

'Why did the chicken cross the road?' I ask her.

'Not now, Katie!' she snaps.

'I'm hungry.' Lilly takes her spoon and throws it to the floor. 'Where's Dad?'

'I don't know.' Mum's voice sounds like it's going to break. Her lip is trembling. I can see she's biting it to stop herself from crying. I do that too.

We start to eat. We are finished and still no Dad. I stack the plates. Mum fiddles with her hair. It's dirty. She hasn't washed it for a week now.

'Do you want me to wash your hair?' I ask her. She starts to laugh – a funny sound.

'Why are you laughing?'

'It's nothing.'

'Is it a joke?'

'No joke – you won't understand.' She starts to pile the dishes in the sink.

'Tell me, I will.' I stand on the kitchen chair so I am at the same height as her head. 'I will understand.' I pull at her hand.

'Don't stand on that chair – I've told you not to. Go on. I can't stand …' she reaches down to slap me, but I dodge her hand. 'Go and lie down before your lessons, and take Lilly with you.'

After lunch we always lie down. Mum lies down a lot. Sometimes it's difficult for her to get up. We have lessons with her in the afternoon. We used to have Miss Berry from England, but she went back. She used to read us stories about a boy whose nails were long and hair was wild and a girl who played with matches and burnt all the children to death. Maria says I'm wild like that girl in the story. At Christmas Miss Berry poured paraffin on the Christmas cake instead of brandy. She thought it would do just as well – just as well!

I drag Lilly with me down the passage to our room. She climbs up onto her bed.

'Go to sleep.' I make a face at her. I lie down and stare at the ceiling. I can't sleep.

I wait until I hear that Mum has stopped moving next door. She is lying on her bed. Lilly is drooling onto her pillow. I tiptoe out of the room and walk down the passage to the kitchen. I am going to find out Mrs Coombe's secret – I know she has one. I open the drawer and take out a teaspoon and put it in my pocket. I am going to find her electricity secret and find what egg she sounds like when she is tapped.

Maria has gone home to clean; her Mum is washing our clothes outside in the yard. I go down to the stables to saddle my pony. I notice that Dad's horse is gone. I ask Philemon if Dad is at the store.

'Baas is gone,' he says.

I have never ridden so far. I am on a quest like King Arthur and the knights into unknown territory and I have planned my route – down along the river that runs through the valley all the way along to the Coombes' farm. I will have to be careful when I get near the farmhouse and hide my pony in the trees and get inside the house without Mrs Coombe seeing me.

My pony stops at the water and I let it drink. I am not thinking of what will happen to me when I get back home – I won't think of that.

When I get to the Coombes' I tie up my pony in the trees. I can't see their car, but perhaps it is parked in the garage at the back. There is no one in the yard. Perhaps they have all left, gone off somewhere and never coming back. I run across the yard. I stop when I come to the stoep. The dog lifts its head. I think it's going to bark. I hold my hand out to its nose and it sniffs me.

The front door is open. I walk inside. It's very still. I can hear someone moving in the kitchen and the sound of pots and pans banging. The bedroom is at the end of the passage. Mrs Coombe always keeps the door closed so you can't tell whether she's inside or not. She keeps her secrets in there. All the way along the passage there are pictures of people staring down from the walls. Watching me.

I am outside her door now. My heart is beating fast. The handle has been polished. It shines in the dark. I wait. I put my ear against the wood. I can hear things. Secret things. The bed is creaking. There is someone in there with her. I can feel the electricity through the door – it shocks my fingers. I hear Mrs Coombe's voice. A cry. There it is, again and again. I don't know what to do – I have to do something. She has to be rescued – perhaps she is being shocked to death, I've read about that. I have to do something. Perhaps I will be a heroine if I save her. I open the door.

There are two bodies on the bed – the electricity must have got them both – they are jerking up and down. I see the back of a man's head and underneath Mrs Coombe's face squashed up against the pillow, all pink. Her hair has come out of the bun she wears. Long pieces stretch across the sheet. I never knew it was so long. They are naked. Their clothes are on the floor. Not tidily arranged but all in a confused jumble, except for a pair of large leather boots – I know those boots.

Mrs Coombe sees me. Her mouth opens. She is hitting the man on the back. She looks at me with wide eyes. He turns his head. 'Katie!'

I turn and run. What is my dad doing there? I run away from the room. I don't know what to do or where to go. I can't work it out – I must work it out. I can hear him shouting after me. 'Katie – come back. I'm sorry! Katie!' Nothing makes sense. He shouldn't have been there – it's not right with his clothes off, jerking up and down like that – like those silly puppets at the fun show – all wrong.

I run away from his voice. My pony is waiting for me under the trees. It is just the same. I climb on and gallop away across the veld away from the thing I don't know. I only stop when I get near the store and hug my pony and wipe my snotty nose against its neck and whisper its name. Where do I go? Back home to Mum? Somewhere safe – the tin church? Will Maria come and find me there?

While I am hesitating, a car arrives. It's Mum. She pulls over in the dirt. I have never seen her driving before. I didn't know she could. She looks wild. 'Where have you been? Where's your Dad?' She grinds the gears and doesn't wait for me to answer. She leaves in a cloud of dust. I know where she's going. I can't stop her. I want to run after her but she's gone. The car is a dot in the dirt.

I go up to the church and wait. Wait for Maria. Wait for Dad to find me and explain about the electricity and Mrs Coombe. I curl up on the pew. Nobody comes. I'm getting hungry.

When I get home Mum and Dad are shouting, walking up and down the sitting room shouting. Lilly is sitting in the corner with a blanket pulled over her head. She's crying.

'Katie,' Dad lifts me up when I come into the room. 'I'm sorry.'

'Sorry!' Mum shouts, and tries to hit him. He puts me down, and follows her down the passage. 'Don't do this.' I can hear him. 'Not in front of them.' I go and sit with Lilly under the blanket. I feel cold now. I don't want to look at Dad. Why did he have to do such a stupid thing? He isn't meant to do things like that – he takes me riding, he teaches me things and now I have seen him like a puppet thing with no clothes.

Mum comes back down the passage with a pile of her clothes. She goes out into the driveway. I run out to see what she's doing. Maria's mum is watching. Maria is watching. Philemon is watching. She throws the clothes down. She has a mad look in her eyes. I have never seen her like this. She has been sleeping all this time and now she's woken up. She goes to the cellar under the house and fetches a can of paraffin. Then she pours it over the clothes. She lights a match and throws it on the pile. It is like the burning bush in the Bible, only the flames are eating Mum's clothes – licking them up.

Dad is running away from the house down towards the stables. I don't know what he's doing. Mum comes back into the house. I follow her into our room. She takes a suitcase down from the cupboard and starts to push our clothes into it. 'What are you doing?' I shout at her.

'We're leaving.'

'What about Dad?'

She mumbles something.

'I can't hear what you're saying!' I shout at her. I am scared now. 'Don't mumble, I can't hear.' I'm crying. 'Miss Berry told us to pronounce our words clearly.' I try again but she doesn't hear me. She's crying now. Crying and pulling us around. My suitcase is full and I haven't even got the important things.

In the morning a car comes to collect us to take us to the train. Dad is going to stop us from going. 'Stop,' I say the words under my breath for him. But he just stands there. He says nothing. He is going to walk over to the driver and talk to him – but he just stands there. The driver has started the car. 'Say it now. Open the door. Take us out.'

Maria just stands there too, like she's forgotten how to speak – with her mouth open she looks so stupid. I lean out of the window and Dad bends his head because he's crying and he doesn't want us to see. And we drive away until they are just tiny dots and I can't see them anymore.

★

They had gone on a boat to England. For most of the trip, Catherine had leant over the ship's railing and stared at the water. She hadn't talked for the whole journey – the words had got stuck in her throat. They had been taken to a place where doors had shut as quickly as they had opened and feet were encased in shoes. No canopy of trees rustling above her head. No crackling dry leaves and dust under her feet. No Dad, no Maria, no river, no prickly pears, no church. She had held the sounds inside her: the wind in the gum trees, the cicadas at night, her father's voice.

She hadn't known then that when she returned to Hebron she would find another man in her father's place.

★ ★ ★

Catherine's feet were getting cold and she took them out of the water and dried them on her blanket. If she waited a bit longer before going to the church Maria would find her. They could go up together. Perhaps it was better that way.

Maria

Maria went out onto the stoep and looked down the driveway and up, past the trees, to the church. The light was still burning. Catherine had left the house and she didn't know how far she had got, but she knew where she was going. It wasn't safe for her out there alone. Catherine had told Maria that fear attracted danger and that she wasn't having any of it. But Maria knew that there were people on the farm who had come from the city with guns. They would see the colour of Catherine's skin – pale in the moonlight. They wouldn't wait for her to speak. If someone surprised Catherine in the dark she was too old to run away.

If she were with her it would be all right. She knew those people – one was the last-born child of her sister. He had come back from across the border because things were changing now – the river was in flood. If she met him on the path she would look him in the eye and he would leave Catherine alone. He would be afraid to do anything in front of his mother's sister. She had her own weapons.

Maria set off with this thought giving her strength, but by the time she reached the gate she had to lean against it to steady herself. Her head was dizzy and her breathing shallow as she fought to get air into her lungs. She knew what was happening: some people had attacks of fear; she had the river bringing her things – uncalled for – washing up in her head. In the dark it stretched wider than she could see, pulling her down under to a place she had forgotten. Now that someone had dug up the bones it was making her remember.

* * *

She is eight-years old; sitting on the wall near the gate chewing on a mango that covers her face and hands with sticky yellow juice.

'Come on, we'll be late!' Katie is pulling at her legs and she jumps down onto the dirt road.

'Does your mother know you come with me?' she asks Katie.

'Don't be stupid, of course she doesn't.'

'You will get in trouble.'

'I don't care. I want to see what you do in the church. I want you to show me.' Katie is already halfway down the road. Maria licks her hands and wipes her face with some leaves then runs to catch up.

The climb up to the church is steep, and it's hot. Maria needs to pee. She can't hold it in. It trickles down, warm and sticky, and her dress sticks to her legs. When they get inside the church they push up against each other in the pew. She can smell the urine and the sweat of her mother sitting next to her. There is singing – a warm breath of it heaving and swaying. She looks up above the altar and waits. And then the vision comes again – because she knows it's a vision now – she read about them in the Bible. Saints had them. She is Saint Maria.

There she is – her aunt who was run over on the road to town – hovering above the altar. Maria thinks of how they took her dead body on the back of a truck to the mortuary where she was wrapped in white, a thin trickle of blood running from her lips, the spirit gone.

But there she is now floating above the priest. Where her face should be, there's a goat's head. The eyes are yellow with black slits. It is like the goat they slaughtered when her eldest brother got married. It stares at her as though it can see right through her. The goat at her brother's wedding had looked at her like that, pleading with her, but she hadn't stopped them from cutting its throat. How could she? The mouth opens. Her aunt is trying to tell her something, but only her lips are moving and a lonely bleating coming out.

'Do you see her?' she turns to Katie, but her friend shakes her head.

'No.'

Maria looks again. Her aunt is gone. They sing from English hymn books in the church. Katie has taught her to read, but she sings from her heart.

'Praise God from where all blessings flow

Praise Him all creatures here below

Praise Him above Ye Heavenly Host Praise Father Son and Holy Ghost … ghost, goat, ghost, goat …'

Perhaps they had sung her aunt there.

They aren't old enough to go up for the communion yet, which is a pity as she likes wine, but the priest blesses them on their heads. Maria's brother keeps turning around in the pew to stare at Katie. Then he reaches out his hand and touches the hair on Katie's arms; he is still amazed at it. Maria slaps his hand and sticks out her tongue. Katie is hers. She is her white friend.

As they file out of the church Maria's mother stands back to let Katie go first. It is like she is a queen or something, the way they treat her, even though she is a child. Queen Catherine King; it makes Maria laugh. Maria is special too. Katie is her friend, she belongs to her. The priest shakes Katie's hand and says he is sorry the sermon was so bad and that his English is so bad. Maria pulls a face. Katie doesn't care. Maria pulls her by the hand. 'Where we going?'

'Into the trees.'

They run away from the congregation, who are filing out into the sunshine. Katie runs after her as she weaves her way between the trees. When she gets to the edge of the cliff, where it plunges down into the pool, she stops and they sit down. Katie picks up a stick and starts scratching in the soil. Maria knows her friend wants to tell her something but she doesn't know how. After a long time Katie looks up at her. Her face is serious. 'Can you see me when I'm not there?' she asks Maria.

'Sometime.'

Maria takes some small rocks in her hand. She throws one over the edge of the cliff down into the pool below, then peers over to watch it land. She throws another in, and counts. 'One, two, three. Let's jump in.' She turns to Katie. But Katie still has that serious look on her face.

'If I get lost, will you know where I am? Will you find me?' She taps Maria on the legs with her stick. Maria picks up a stick and they start to fight with them.

'You don't get lost.' Maria laughs, knocking Katie's stick out of her hand.

'But if I do?'

Katie is standing up. She looks down into the pool below. 'Let's take off our clothes.' She is unbuttoning her dress.

'And then?'

'Smear ourselves with mud at the pool.'

'Like boys?'

'Yes. Then we'll go inside the church.'

'And do what?'

'We'll know when we get inside.'

'So that you don't get lost.'

But Katie had got lost. Maria had watched from the driveway as her friend was driven away in a black car that got further and further away until it was just a dot in the dust. Maria had tried to find her.

When her friend had gone, the river had come to her carrying on it things – forgotten things, things whispered in the breeze off the water, things washed up and left glistening in her small hands.

It let her see what had happened and what was going to happen. She had felt her mother crying in the veld and gone out to find her with a broken leg. She knew when it was going to rain or when someone was in trouble.

The river was there wherever she went. Just below her, just above her. When she lay in the smoky hut and stared at the clay ceiling. When she chased chickens, when she was cleaning in the house at Hebron. It was the river that brought Katie back to her.

Mr King left the farm a year after Katie was taken away. It was 1932 when he packed a suitcase one day and just drove off, leaving all the furniture in the house. He told Maria that a manager would come to look after the farm for him. But when she had asked him if he was going to find Katie he had looked away from her. There had been no letter from Katie, not that Maria had seen. At night she had seen Mr King sitting out on the stoep – she felt his loneliness like an empty space without light.

Before he left, the congregation had stopped worshipping in the tin church, because he had built them a new church on the other side of the road from the store – a native church. Now the old women and men who worked on the farms didn't have to climb the steep slope in the heat.

The tin church belonged to her now.

After Mr King left, Maria took a photograph of Katie that she found in the house up to the tin church and hung it on the wall. She put their mugs, one blue, one red, beneath it on the floor, together with the picture book that Katie had used to teach her to read. Then she ran down among the trees to the edge of the cliff and looked over at the pool below.

There was a hole so big in her heart that if she stood at the edge and threw things down she couldn't hear them hit the bottom.

She ran back up the hill into the church and closed her eyes. She could hear Katie's laughter. It spun her head. If she reached out her hand she could feel her fingers pulling her. The water was rising; she felt dizzy. She could see her friend, clearer than a dream.

Katie was standing on a beach. It was cold and the sky was grey. She was naked and her skin looked blue. She started to run towards the water but her mum came running across the sand and took her by the arm. Katie tried to hit her – her arms were flapping like small wings. She was crying. Maria called out to her but Katie couldn't hear. Then she was gone.

Maria knelt down and waited with her eyes closed but she couldn't see anything more. Her mother found her curled up on the floor of the tin church and took her back home.

★

She grew into a skinny teenager; watching managers come and go at Hebron. Some of them didn't see her at all, they moved past her. Some of them had wives who made her clean and polish. One of them gave her books to read. Another tried to push her skirt up and stick his penis inside her, but she scratched his face. None of them lasted long. It was as if the house chewed them up and spat them out like a bitter taste.

And there were boys. Boys who followed her around like scrawny dogs, boys who charged at her like bulls, boys who slunk around like the cats or fluffed out their feathers like the cockerels in the yard. She charged the boys a shilling to kiss her in the sitting room at Hebron, and more to take them into the church and show them her friend and read to them from the picture book. They were frightened of her because she was different from them. She could understand the white people who came and went, everything they said, and she could speak to them too in their language.

Whenever she could she would go up to the church and stand with her eyes shut, waiting. But she didn't see Katie again on the river in her mind until she was seventeen and the war had started.

It was a war far away in Europe and England. She had read about it in a newspaper down at the railway siding. She had asked the Indian shopkeeper and he had told her it was the second time such a big war had happened in the world. And she had thought it was too far away – it wouldn't touch them. But then the manager at Hebron had gone off to fight in North Africa and the trucks had rattled past on the road carrying soldiers who were going off to join him.

When Katie appeared to her in the church, it was the night of her middle brother's coming-home party. He had been at mountain school, covered in clay like her and Katie. When he came down the mountain dressed in smart clothes he had become a man. They slaughtered a goat and there was dancing. That was the night that Maria met a man she loved. He wasn't like the other boys. He was quiet and interesting and when she teased him he just gave her a sweet smile. When he touched her she didn't push his hands away. She didn't have to scratch him or threaten him; he didn't try to force her. She ran in the dark up to the church and stood at the altar and waited. The water rose up her legs. It was warm this time, the sun was shining, and the grey clouds had gone.

Katie was sitting in sand dunes in amongst tufts of grass, busy with something. A man was sitting next to her. He had a boyish face but he sat like an old man, hunched over a sketchbook. A dog was lying on the sand with its head pressed up against Katie. She was stroking its head with one hand; in the other she had a paintbrush.

Maria leaned over her shoulder so that she could see what Katie was painting on the small canvas that rested on her lap. The young man looked up; he stared right through Maria. Then he looked back at the thing he was studying, something that he held in his hand. An urchin thing. Maria had seen one like it at Hebron, in the book on marine life – which was life of things in the sea.

There was paint on Katie's face where her brush had touched her skin and paint on her skirt and in her hair. The man leaned across and wiped the paint off her skin with a handkerchief. Maria looked down at the canvas. There was the church – silver in the moonlight.

Maria touched her shoulder and Katie turned around and stared at her.

When the river had gone she looked up and saw the man with the sweet smile from the party. He was standing in the entrance. As she walked towards him she felt something separating, pulling away as he drew her in.

They lay on a boulder under the stars until the sun came up and he held her hand. He was the man she loved, the man who opened doors inside her and let the warm wind in, and the man who brought her home. And he was the man who left. He went back on the truck to the city, to the mines. He died there. They brought his body back and buried him in the graveyard behind the tin church.

The river brought him to Maria as she lay on the dusty floor in front of the pews. It brought him to her on a black current of water; he was floating, his legs were crushed.

She thought of what she and Katie had wished for that day in the church, all painted with mud. She felt her young body lying there on the floor and knew it should be lying next to his alive and warm and she thought of all the things that she had wanted to show him.

For the first month she took him bread and beer and mushrooms from the veld, laying them down on his gravestone. She sat for hours with him, sleeping at night in the church. After a month she went back to Hebron and she stopped. She just stopped.

For the next month she spent the days sitting in the driveway outside the house at Hebron on a blanket in the sun. Her sister started cleaning in the house. At night she would move her blanket onto the stoep, and the next morning back into the driveway. She didn't talk to anyone. When she did get up and start cleaning in the house, it was like she was moving in a dream.

The years slid by and the war got closer to them.

It was fighting that brought her back. It stirred the edges of her stillness. People coming and going. Trucks rattling by on the dirt road. The manager of the farm came back from North Africa with things from faraway places that she had only read about: camel bags and silver coffee pots.

Then the Italians arrived. The prisoners of war. They came to work on the farm. They wouldn't leave Maria alone to sit on her blanket. Every day one of them would sit down in front of her in the sand and sing to her in a funny language and tell her she was pretty. He would pinch her until she stood up and started to move around again. In all this time she hadn't seen Katie because she hadn't been to the church.

At the end of the war the Italians left and Maria went to the church again.

Katie was sitting at a table with the man from the beach. There was a candle on the table and through the window Maria could see the lights of boats in the dark. The man handed Catherine something, a small box. He was smiling. She opened the box; there was a ring inside. It sparkled on the dark velvet. Maria knew what that meant and she shouted, but Katie was putting it on her finger, twisting it this way and that.

⋆ ⋆ ⋆

Maria stirred. She lifted herself up off the ground. She had come out to look for Catherine and been surprised by the past. She started down the avenue and followed the path behind the school. Where the path split to go up to the church she bent down and ran her fingers over the earth. There were two sets of footprints. One was Catherine's; the other was larger, a man's.

Hendrik

Hendrik had walked to Hebron in the late afternoon, but something had stopped him from going up to the house. He had turned back and followed the path down to the river and up to the church where he had waited until it was dark and then lit the paraffin lamps. He had waited but Catherine hadn't come and he was worried that his wife would be anxious alone on their farm. He walked fast and didn't stop at the passage through the rocks that led to the burial site, but continued down the slope. His job at the church was done.

The first time he had walked this path, all the way to the church, he had been twelve years old. That day he had looked up at the church and for the first time wondered what happened up there.

⋆ ⋆ ⋆

'What is it?' he asked his Pa out in the yard where they were fixing a fence.

'It's a kaffir church,' he told him. 'They go up there to worship, not our God though. You aren't to go there.' Hendrik didn't know why he had said this.

'Whose land is it on?'

'Mr King's land. It's on Hebron.'

'Mr King who left?'

But his Pa went inside the house to fetch another pair of pliers, and his Ma was calling him. She was sitting on the stoep; she had been there all morning. 'Bring me a glass of water and my pills, my head is hurting me.' She eased herself in the chair. Every day she had a migraine and every day they heard about it. It sat on Hendrik's chest like a heavy weight.

He was an only child.

He brought her the glass of water and pills. 'You're a good boy. You know that don't you?' She took his hand and squeezed it. 'Come and sit here, Ma se kind. If I'm feeling better later I'll bake a cake, would you like that?'

'I'd like that, Ma.'

'Your teacher tells me you're doing well at school. Have you got any homework?'

'Ma, can I ride over to the Duke's farm this afternoon?'

'Hendrik, it's too far, you know it's dangerous down by the river. I don't want you riding down there. Anyway the ladies from the church are coming for coffee and cakes. Wouldn't it be nice to see them?'

'Can I go on the weekend?'

She hesitated. 'Hendrik, they are English. They support the English.'

'But Ma.'

When the ladies came in the afternoon he sat in the corner listening. They were talking about Hebron.

'The meid just sits in the driveway all day. Nobody tells her to move. I can't understand it. I would beat some sense into her.' Mrs De Vries leant across for another scone. Hendrik watched the flour stick to the fluff on her chin.

'She's waiting for her friend to come back. Mr King's daughter. The mother used to let her go with the natives, she ran wild. She even went up to the church. She used to worship with them, if you can call it worship.'

Something jumped inside Hendrik. This white girl had been up to the church – a girl his age. She had gone to the church.

'What happened to the girls?'

'Mother took them back to England. She never liked it here; she was born in England. They say she never came out of the house. Daughter discovered the father with another woman.'

Hendrik always wondered who *they* were, when the ladies talked *they* say this, *they* say that.

'What happened to the Pa?'

'He left the farm. *They* say he went down to the coast, became a drunk. Sends managers to run the farm but they all leave. There's something about that house if you ask me.'

'And the mother and the girls never came back?'

'No. You can't blame them, can you?'

The next day on the bus to school Hendrik sat with his head pressed up against the window. James Duke, his English friend, didn't take the bus anymore because the Afrikaans boys had tried to hang him by his tie. Hendrik had lifted him up and unhooked the tie so that he could breathe again.

The bus was driving down the avenue of gum trees, past the store. The boy next to him pulled at his shirtsleeve. 'Look.' He was pointing out of the window. Two men were digging in the garden at Hebron. Their skin was dark brown in the sun. One of them had a monkey on his shoulder. A native girl was sitting in the driveway watching them.

'Italians!' The boys in the bus cheered and waved at them. 'Prisoners of war.'

At school Hendrik went to the library. He took out an atlas and found Italy. He traced his finger over the desert in North Africa where the Italians were captured. After school he drove with his father down to the railway siding. The Italian man with the monkey was in the store buying food. He asked him what the monkey's name was.

'Toto,' the man told him. Hendrik's Pa took his hat off and nodded his head; they were on the same side, he was saying. Hendrik didn't want to be on a side. They watched the British convoys passing on their way up into the mountains. The boys threw stones at the trucks, the boys who tried to hang his friend. He joined in.

That night he packed a bag. He could hear his Pa snoring next door. He climbed out of his window and lowered himself down onto the ground. As he ran across the veld, he got lighter and lighter. His Ma's voice became a faint echo. When he got to the koppies he lay down on a rock and stretched his arms out. It felt like he was swimming in the moonlight. Perhaps he wouldn't go back to the house. He could find a cave in the rocks and live off water from the river and plants, like Jesus in the wilderness. The sky was a mass of stars. They were icy pinpricks in the blackness and below them was the black of the land and the pinpricks of lights from farmhouses. Perhaps he was upside down; which was heaven and which was earth? He heard something rustling in the grasses nearby and sat up. A shiver ran across his skin, but it was only a *vlakhaas*, darting off into the rocks.

There was a rough path and he followed it up between the koppies. He was just underneath the church when he stopped, in the shadows. Someone was moving about outside, behind the church. His eyes became used to the dark and he saw that it was the native girl from Hebron. She was sitting on one of the graves with a blanket wrapped around her shoulders, rocking gently back and forth. He thought she heard him, because she turned around and looked into the darkness. After a long time she got up and moved off.

He came out of his hiding place and stretched his legs that were stiff from crouching. He felt his way over the rocks up to the church. The door was open and he slid inside. Someone had left a candle burning. He saw the photograph on the wall and he knew it was her – the white girl from Hebron who had to leave to go back to England, who used to worship in the church with the natives. She was smiling at him; there was a gap between her teeth. It was just her head and shoulders in the photograph so he couldn't see how big she was. Underneath the photograph, on the floor, he found the picture book. He opened it and shone his torch on the first page. A name was written in black ink.

Catherine.

Now he knew who she was. When he met her he could call her by her name.

⋆ ⋆ ⋆

The lights were off when Hendrik reached the farmhouse. The dogs barked and ran up to him, but he stroked their heads to quieten them and they pressed themselves against his legs.

After he had married he had moved back to this house, his parents' house, the house where he had grown up. His father had got sick and they had come to nurse him. He had died a year later and was buried next to Hendrik's mother in a small cemetery on the farm. Hendrik walked quietly down the passage. He stopped outside his daughter's room. She had left home when she was eighteen – two years after Tom Fyncham had died and two years after he had gone back to Hebron to visit Catherine to see if she needed help. Now his daughter lived in town with a family of her own.

His wife was still asleep when he entered their room. Her breathing was even, in and out, in and out. A breeze blew the curtains and the light material shuddered in the moonlight. Out of the window the night world was bright. From where they slept he could see across the land and up to the ridge where the church stood. The lights were still burning. He wondered how long it would take Catherine to get there and if she would like what he had left for her in the church. He thought of the years he had waited for her to return to Hebron – years when he hadn't been up to the church. When it had been used for other things. And all that time Hendrik had watched what happened at Hebron from a distance.

Part Two

One

It was 1952. The years after the war had slid past Maria in the heat of the summers and the icy cold of the winter nights and early mornings and Maria turned twenty-nine without knowing it. It felt like she had been in a long sleep, that her dreams were interrupted by the daytime and fed by the books she read. The last manager had left six months ago. The garden at Hebron was overgrown with weeds. Creepers had grown up the walls of the house and slates had tumbled off the roof. One of the palm trees that stood on either side of the front steps had been struck by lightning and the top had fallen off. The curtains in the house were shut to the outside world. The workers had gone to work on the neighbouring farms. Only Gabriel still grew vegetables in the garden up at the house and kept his goats at the back.

After the war Maria had moved into one of the rooms off the central courtyard as the caretaker. The last manager had left her the keys to Hebron saying that as caretaker she was responsible for the house until the next manager came. She kept the keys around her neck on a piece of leather – but no one arrived. As far as she was concerned the house was hers. Although she still went to visit her mother and told her about the things she had read, she always went back to Hebron. She had a place of her own – a big house full of books. Every morning she woke up early, lit the stove in the kitchen, and made tea and porridge for herself and Gabriel. They would sit outside the kitchen on a bench in the sun. Gabriel would make sucking noises when he drank his tea; he did it on purpose to annoy her. After they had finished eating she would turn him out of the house and lock the kitchen door so that he couldn't spy on her. He had asked her again and again what she did all day in the house, but she wouldn't tell him.

When she was sure that he had taken his spade and gone off to work in the vegetable garden she would take a feather duster and unlock the door to the sitting room. It was a large, L-shaped room with a fireplace in the short arm of the 'L'. A long mirror hung on the wall next to the front door. The centrepiece of the room was a gramophone. Maria had pulled it away from the wall, out into the middle of the carpet. She would choose a record and place it on the turntable. She liked to wind the handle of the gramophone and watch the needle scratching the surface of the record, releasing the sound from the grooves. There were sounds hidden in the cracks. Over the years, farm managers and their wives had left records and books behind. Maria liked to listen to Edmundo Ross's Latin American Big Band. It was music from another world that was hot and bright and full of laughter. When the record finished she would start to dust, flicking the duster lightly over the top of the grand piano, along the bookshelves that lined the walls and over the ornaments. She would even dust herself in the mirror. Then she would put the duster down on the mantelpiece, sit on the floor in front of the bookshelf and start to read.

In the mornings in the quiet of the house she mapped out trails across continents, she read about the stars, the desert, sexual diseases, how to grow roses, varieties of poisonous snakes.

On the morning of the day that Mr Fyncham arrived at Hebron, Maria pulled *The Return of the Native* from the bookshelf. In it she discovered a woman called Eustacia, who went out onto the land and stood with her back to the wind. She was lonely. She looked through a telescope in the dark, searching for someone to love. Maria left the book open on the floor and ran out into the sunshine in the courtyard. Something had echoed down through her skin and found her heart.

Gabriel found her there, huddled up against the wall. He told her that he'd been calling her for ten minutes and she hadn't answered. 'You never listen,' he complained. When she heard it was a cup of tea he wanted she told him to leave her alone and make it himself. Then she went into her room, took the old grey blanket off her bed and went out onto the driveway where she lay the blanket down under the peach tree and settled down to sleep.

At lunch she went back into the house to get the sheep's ribs and pap she had cooked the night before. She ate out in the sun. The meat was tasty and she mopped the gravy up with mealie meal and licked it off her fingers. Everything was slow in the heat. When she had stripped the ribs she lay down to sleep. It was when she closed her eyes that she became conscious of a noise out on the road.

A car was coming down the hill. The sound of the engine didn't fit any of the trucks and tractors she knew. It was smoother, it purred. There was jazz music playing on the car radio. The notes shimmered in the heat, rushing up and down, jumping this way and that – shattering the stillness, stirring up the dust.

The car skidded to a halt in front of the house. She smelt the oil and petrol in the heat off the engine. Never before had she seen such a big car or such a smart one. It was covered in red dust, but the black paintwork gleamed through.

The first thing she saw of Mr Fyncham when he got out of the car were his shoes. They were black and shiny like the car, not the shoes of a farmer but the shoes of someone from the city. He was wearing khaki trousers and a white shirt that was unbuttoned in the heat, showing his chest, the colour of honey. He was older than she was, ten years older, she thought. Ten was a good number. He was the most handsome white man Maria had ever seen. His face had character, he had lines from laughing and the sun, but it was the way he looked around him. He stared out past the house and down to the stables that were falling down, seeing more than was there, mapping things, changing the future. He was like one of those explorers she had seen photographs of in her books –

men who discovered new lands and crossed them and left their wives at home for years to look after the children.

There was someone else in the car, a woman, and for a second Maria thought it was Katie. That she had found this man somewhere out there and brought him back to Hebron. But the woman who got out of the car was nothing like her friend. This woman had hair that was black and glossy like a starling's feathers. It was brushed smooth and held back by a silver clasp. Catherine had never owned a brush; she had combed the knots out of her hair with her fingers. Sometimes she would twirl her hair and tie it with bits of string, other times Maria would plait it for her. They would sit in the sun playing with each other's hair or tickling each other's backs with grasses. Catherine's hair shone with copper and gold.

This woman's skin was olive and her eyes were dark, like sinkholes. You would struggle to tread water in that darkness. Her full lips were painted deep red and she was wearing a pale green summer dress that was tight at the waist and stretched over her full breasts and the curve of her hips.

The man and woman stood and stared at the house. They didn't see Maria sitting under the tree. She was black, she was a shadow, invisible to them.

'Well, what do you think?' the woman turned to the man. 'I didn't think it would be this big. I thought he was exaggerating when he said it had so many rooms.' There was triumph in her voice, as though she'd won the house in a competition and was showing the man her prize. The way she spoke English was different to any accent Maria had heard around the farm. She didn't sound like anyone Maria knew or had met, but she had heard a voice like that before somewhere, it was familiar.

'Is it how you thought?' The woman walked over to where the man stood and rested her fingers on his arm, stroking the skin lightly. 'It's all ours now.'

Maria saw him flinch. She saw his shoes moving in the dust. He shook his head. 'You can say it's yours, but I ...'

'We're in this together, Tom. Come on. Now is not the time to doubt. Not when we've come this far.'

He was still staring at the house. Maria looked at it too. She wondered what the houses were like where they came from, and she realised that she didn't know whether this house was different from houses out there beyond the farms. It wasn't like the other farmhouses in the district, but then the Kings hadn't been like the other farmers either.

'Come on. There's been nothing from England. They never came back did they? And if they do – well it's too late isn't it.' The woman bent down and slapped at a fly that had landed on her calf.

Maria moved out of the shadows. They turned, saw her, and stared.

Maria wondered if her clothes were on back to front, she hadn't bothered to look in the mirror that morning, and Gabriel would have let her go out in the street naked, just so that he could laugh. She stood up. The man approached her, holding out his hand.

'Mr Fyncham.'

Maria nodded but stayed standing where she was, at some distance from him.

'This is my wife.'

The woman was looking at Maria warily as if she were a wild animal that might bite. 'We've bought the farm. Are those the keys to the house?' Mr Fyncham pointed to the keys around her neck and then to the house in case she couldn't understand him. Maria put her hand over them protectively. They wouldn't explain anything to her. Where they had come from, who they were, why there was no manager, where Mr King was. She was a servant.

'Tell her to help us with the suitcases.' The woman walked to the back of the car, opened the boot and waited. Mr Fyncham looked like he was going to say something but changed his mind and went to the boot and started to take the suitcases out.

'Let the girl do it,' she said impatiently. 'It's too hot. I need a drink.'

She scrabbled in her bag and pulled out a crumpled packet of cigarettes, shook one out and lit it. 'What is she waiting for?' she said loudly, staring at Maria, who walked to the car and ran her fingers along the side, leaving a wavy trail in the dust. The man looked up from where he had the suitcases lined up on the ground. 'Is there a boy who can wash the car?'

Maria nodded again. She didn't trust herself to speak. Gabriel must have gone off early because he wasn't there when she turned to the garden.

The Fynchams had a lot of suitcases. They were all different sizes but all were made of dark green leather and they looked as if they cost a lot of money. The smallest one was the size of a shoebox. Maria wondered what anyone would carry in such a small suitcase. There was a box of bottles still in the boot and she started pulling them out one by one and reading the labels. Gin, tonic, wine, whisky … it was a long time since she had had a drink from a bottle. The Italians had given her cheap wine.

'What are you doing? Put those back,' the woman had come up behind her. She crushed out her cigarette butt with the heel of her black leather sandals. 'Do you understand what I'm saying?'

Maria ignored this, picked up two suitcases and walked towards the house. The man was following with more of the cases.

She stopped when she came to the front door, put the suitcases down and hesitated. This was the end of her world alone inside the house. But there was nothing she could do. She took the keys from around her neck and unlocked the door. Edmundo Ross and his big band vanished – they fled out the back along with the light and heat and colour of their world. The man and woman walked past her into the sitting room; keen to see what was now theirs, what they had bought.

Maria listened to the click-click of the woman's heels on the wooden floorboards as she walked down the passage flinging open doors, disturbing the dust, crushing the thin wings of the flying insects that had collected on the floor. *Trespassers will be prosecuted*. Maria had seen the sign on the gate of the next-door farm. She should have put one on the front door. Trespassers will be strung up in the prickly pear tree – because she felt they were trespassing. They didn't belong here. There had been no word from Mr King. Nothing to say he wasn't coming back, that he had sold the farm.

She stood as still as she could in the corner by the fireplace. Her eyes were the only part of her that moved as they followed the man around the room. He opened the lid of the piano and ran his fingers over the keys. Then he saw the pile of books on the floor. There was no time for Maria to cross the room and pick them up; he was already bending down and picking up the book she had been reading.

'*Return of the Native*.' He said the title out loud and then he looked up at Maria, puzzled. 'Are you reading this?'

She hesitated then nodded her head. He didn't believe her, how could she be reading such a book.

'*Far from the Madding Crowd* … have you read that?' He was teasing her now. He was looking straight at her and she looked straight back, unflinching.

'No.' It came out hoarse and she coughed to clear her throat. 'No. I haven't,' she said more clearly.

'What's this then?' He held up another book to the light. '*Animal Husbandry*. Eclectic taste in books.'

Eclectic, electric? Eclectric? – she searched for the word but couldn't find it; she would have to look it up.

He walked around the room examining things. He came close to her and she tried to lean backwards so that they wouldn't touch each other when he leant over to pick up a small wooden box next to her on the mantelpiece. For some reason she couldn't move her feet.

She watched as he blew the dust off the lid, opened the box and emptied the contents onto his hand. He had beautiful hands, not fleshy like Gabriel's or sweaty like the man at the railway siding. She wanted to touch them.

The emerald beetle shimmered in the light from the window. He held it up. 'All this in the middle of nowhere, who would have thought?' And she knew he meant her as well as the contents of the house. An educated native who could speak English like the queen.

Her eyebrows lifted and she swayed slightly with the effort of speaking.

'Mr King? How is Mr King?'

He turned to face her. She couldn't read his expression because he made his face go still like a mask. 'He's dead. He died two months ago.'

'I didn't know. Does …' but then she stopped. She didn't want to say Katie's name in front of him or his wife, but she would have to because Mr Fyncham was looking at the portrait of Katie above the mantelpiece. He stood and examined it for a long time and Maria knew then that he had seen Katie before. But he turned to her.

'Who is the portrait of?' he asked.

It was a direct question; she would have to answer. She cleared her throat.

'That is Catherine. Mr King's daughter.'

He leant closer to see the signature. 'Mr King painted it himself. I didn't know he painted.' Then he drew back to look at it from a distance. 'She's lovely.' He said it quietly.

He was standing in front of the portrait when his wife came back into the room. 'What are you staring at?' Her voice was laughing, but scornful. Her reaction to the painting was different; her mouth became a thin bitter line. She ran her fingers along the mantelpiece. 'This place is dirty.' He hadn't heard her; he was frowning at the picture as though he was trying to remember something.

'Oh stop staring. It's only a picture. She's not here you know. Anyway, I think it's very amateur – in fact the whole house is in very bad taste, and so dirty. What's the girl been doing? Whatever it is it's not cleaning.'

'She's been reading,' Mr Fyncham said. He winked at Maria and she didn't know what to do.

'We want drinks. Two gin and tonics, is there ice?' the woman spoke loudly and slowly. 'You have ice for drinks?'

'She speaks English. Probably better than you do.' Mr Fyncham didn't face his wife when he spoke; he walked away from her across the room and took one of the suitcases through into the study.

'Well, don't just stand there, get drinks then.' She gestured to the door.

'There are no ice trays.' Maria's voice was coming back; it wasn't a whisper any more.

'Tea then, whatever.' The woman slumped down in an armchair and pulled off her sandals. Her toenails were painted a deep crushed purple red, the colour of mulberries on the tree at the back of the house – deep red like thick blood. Katie and Maria had climbed the tree to pick the berries. Katie's skin was stained red. They had crept down the passage to where Lilly was playing with her toys. Katie had jumped out in front of her, froth on her lips, clutching her heart.

Help me.

Lilly had screamed. They had laughed.

Mrs Fyncham's pouty lips were the same crushed mulberry colour. When Maria came back with the tea, Mr Fyncham was looking through one of their suitcases. It was full of books and papers and lots of maps. So he *was* an explorer. She wanted to ask him where he had been – for him to tell her about the places she read about. But she didn't have a chance because the woman was already complaining. 'The tea tastes funny.' She looked at Maria accusingly as if she had done it deliberately. And then she started with the orders. 'I want you to clean everything, properly. Take the suitcases down to the bedroom at the end of the passage. The one on the left, it has the best view. Clean in there too, properly. There's a box of food in the car. Cook us pasta for supper – there are tins you can use for sauce.'

In the evening they sat in the courtyard. The air was warm. Mrs Fyncham had changed into a flowery gown and her make-up looked fresh. She flicked through a magazine with her mulberry nails while her husband read a book on farming. It had pictures of different breeds of cows and sheep. If he had asked her, Maria could have told him all of them, naming them, giving him the best regions for each breed, how to kill the pests that infested them, which were meat and which dairy or wool. She thought of asking him for a cigarette, but changed her mind. The woman would not allow it. Mr Fyncham was intelligent and different from his wife, too different Maria thought. He had seen a lot of things and learned a great deal. But if his wife decided she wanted a new servant who didn't talk back, who didn't know too much, they would send Maria away from the house and she wanted to stay. She had got used to living there. Things would change now. The way it had been – reading the books, inviting her family over to come and eat in the big kitchen, playing music on the gramophone. All that would stop now they had come. All she could do was try and stay there so that she was there when Katie came home.

She sat waiting for them to finish so that she could take the plates away. They didn't speak to each other. The woman kept folding the corners of pages in the magazine. She would hold up a picture of curtains or bed linen for her husband to look at but he wasn't interested.

'I'm going to start in the sitting room. All the pictures must come down.' Her voice was high, it cut the night air.

He went on reading. Mrs Fyncham tossed the magazine down and stood up. 'You can go now,' she told Maria. 'We'll have coffee in the morning. Bring it to the bedroom.' He didn't look up. Was this how he coped with her?

When they were sleeping Maria walked around the house in the dark, touching the walls. She went to stand by the gramophone and turned the handle. There was no record on the turntable. Then she fetched a bag, emptied some books from the shelves and slid Edmundo Ross in behind them. 'I'm going to the church,' she told Katie. 'I'll see you there.' She said it as if they met there every night, as though if she said it lightly like this then there would be no question about it.

She liked walking in the dark because she could slide into the shadows and watch as people passed walking home. She liked knowing that she could see them but they couldn't see her. When she got to the church she would hide the books somewhere, so that she could go on reading. The new people couldn't stop her. It was her life. It was what made her different from Gabriel.

As though she had summoned him just by thinking of him, he appeared in front of her on the path. She could smell the beer on his breath, and his sweat. He grabbed her around the waist before she could run.

'Where are you going?' he asked her. 'Are you running away?' His hands were rough. 'Take me with you.'

'There's a new baas at Hebron and he asked where you were.' She knew he would be annoyed not to be the first to know. Not to be the one who informed her.

He looked dazed. Maria could see what she had said making its way slowly into a thought in that great thick skull. Then he tried to grab her again.

'Where are you going?'

But she pushed him away. He was gone and she was out on the path again. Her body felt light, out in the veld, and she realised how heavy she had got in the house. It was like when she closed the doors to the gramophone and the sound was muffled, that's how she had been. But out here the doors were open and the sound was clear. She started to run. She was young and thin and pretty. There was a handsome man in the house. The sky was dotted with stars. There had been a big bang. She started humming a tune, bringing her voice back from the place it had been resting. When she reached the river she lay down to smell the earth and feel the grass against her skin. Then she crawled on her hands and knees for a few yards to see how the world looked from that angle – like a hare or a small buck. She laughed. It was no wonder they thought she was crazy. She got up and climbed the path to the church.

The door was propped open with a rock and the moonlight lit up a pathway across the floor to the wooden table that had been used as an altar. She lay down on the floor.

★

Hendrik ran across the veld and up through the koppies to the church. He was seventeen and fit. He could run all the way without stopping, like a long-distance runner. When he got to the church he saw that someone had shut the door. He moved to the window and peered in. It was the black girl from Hebron. She was lying on the floor. Her eyes were closed. She looked dead but then he saw her hand move, just a slight flicker. He stood and watched her. He would have to wait until she had left before he could go inside.

Maria called the river up this time.

The wind was blowing hard and the sky was dark. She didn't know where she was but she could taste salt on her lips and water in the air. There were stones under her feet, round smooth ones. As she stood there she became aware of a flapping sound; something was caught in the wind. She moved slowly towards the noise. Now she could hear the sound of water on rocks below her. Katie was standing; leaning out into the wind that was holding her up. If it stopped blowing so hard she would fall onto the rocks below. She had a suitcase next to her. She was coming home.

Two

Every morning for the next week Maria went out to the gate and stared down the drive, expecting Katie to come walking down the avenue with her suitcase. But there was no sign of her.

The early mornings were the only time Maria had left to herself because as soon as Mrs Fyncham woke up she kept Maria busy, cleaning and cooking and washing – there was no time for her to sit and read or escape up to the church.

Mr Fyncham would go out early, often before his wife woke up. He would get his own breakfast and Maria would take his lunch down into the veld to where he was working. He would come back late and then he would read.

She watched him in the evenings when he read or studied his maps. His wife would call from the bedroom trying to get him to join her. When she was asleep Mr Fyncham would ask Maria to bring him a drink and he would stay up until two or three in the morning. In this time Maria began to read again. He would let her sit up with him in the sitting room or on the stoep if it was hot.

Mrs Fyncham was the one who gave Maria orders. Mr Fyncham was the one who talked to her. He wanted to know who had taught her to speak such perfect English, how she had got to be so clever, and why she didn't have a boyfriend. He asked her all about Katie. It was as though he couldn't hear enough. What did they use to do together, where did they go on the farm, which were their favourite places? Had Katie played the piano? What had she been like? And she started to tell him things.

At the end of the month Mr Fyncham had got all the workers back onto the farm and he had paid them all. Maria had gone down to the store and bought sugar, a large bag of it, and mealie meal, to take to her mother.

With his energy Mr Fyncham brought the farm back to life. He got the tractor working and fixed the pump and fenced off the fields. He started a school for the workers' children in one of the buildings at the store, and got a black teacher from town to come and teach. It was a good thing he had done, Maria thought. The children would have books; they would be able to read.

At the end of the day he would come back to the house, tired but satisfied as things began to take shape and look the way he had seen them. As the farm came back to life the tension in him began to ease. Maria heard him laughing one morning while he was talking to Gabriel outside the kitchen and she knew that he was beginning to love the place, the land, the river, the hills, the trees. That he had made them his and he didn't want to leave.

Mrs Fyncham didn't want to stay in the house. Maria could see that. She was restless and lonely. In that first month she took the car and went to town often, coming back late having spent the day shopping. The car would come flying into the drive as though she wanted an accident to happen, something to change the way things were. She bought new plates, knives, forks, glasses, linen for their bed and things for the bathroom. And always a box filled with bottles of drink: whisky, gin, tonic … She would be all lit up when she came back from these trips and would talk about changing this and changing that and about a dress she had seen or a bag or hat she must have. And then after half an hour she would slump in a chair and ask for her drink and snap at Maria.

One day she came back with a new record. She had found a song she liked, she told Maria. It was *their* favourite song, she said. When Mr Fyncham came home she made him dance with her. Maria thought of Edmundo Ross pressed between the cold sleeves of the record cover, silent in the church. Mr Fyncham was a good dancer. If he had asked Maria to dance he would have seen what a good dancer she was too. It was the only time Maria saw Mr Fyncham touch his wife. But Mrs Fyncham was difficult; perhaps he didn't want to get too close to her. Her moods changed so quickly and once she threw a vase across the room. It nearly hit him and he grabbed her wrist, tightly. Maria could see that it really hurt. In that moment he hated her, Maria could see it in his face.

In the second month Mrs Fyncham lost interest in shopping and Maria twice found her standing in front of the portrait of Katie, staring at it. She had wanted to get between her and the painting, to shield Katie from those dark eyes.

Mrs Fyncham started to stay in bed later and later until one day she hadn't got up by lunchtime. Maria put slices of cold meat onto a tray and made a salad. Mrs Fyncham normally oversaw lunch, making Maria wash every lettuce leaf and rearrange the tomatoes, but today Maria was alone in the kitchen. She watched the tiny slugs wriggling down the lettuce leaves as she arranged them in the salad bowl. Colours were important – she heard Mrs Fyncham's voice in her head, in that funny way she spoke English. You can't have it like this – her fingernails a different shade every day. Maria, change the colours, see: carrots first, orange, then red, then green – she had seen it in a magazine.

Maria had seen her rubbing at the skin on the side of her index finger where she held the cigarettes, trying to get the yellow stain off. One day she rubbed so hard with a pumice stone that her finger bled. The next day she got a cigarette holder but the stains on her fingers were ingrained, she couldn't get them off. She smoked all the time. Her fingers were always moving – if they weren't lighting a cigarette, they were in and out of the many bottles on her dressing table. She was terrified of getting old – it was funny, Maria thought, because she was beautiful and young, beautiful in the way that the women in the magazines were. But she would look in the mirror and frown and push her waist in and pinch the flesh on her arms.

Maria made a circle with tomatoes and stuck two radishes in the center. Between them she placed a carrot, poking upwards. It made her laugh.

After she had eaten pap and meat in the kitchen she wiped the grease off her fingers on her skirt, put a piece of netting over the food and took the tray down the passage. She put it down on the floor outside their bedroom so that she could knock on the door.

There was no answer and she knocked again. Then she opened the door. Mrs Fyncham was sitting on the edge of the bed holding her stomach. She was bent double. Her face was pale. She looked up as Maria came in. 'Get out,' she hissed through her teeth. Then she pushed Maria aside as she ran to the bathroom and retched into the toilet. Her hair was wet from sweat. Maria moved forward to help her but she held out her arm to keep her away. 'I said, keep out.' There was a trickle of saliva running down her chin.

Maria took the tray back to the kitchen. She went out onto the driveway to call for Mr Fyncham, but Gabriel said he'd taken the car to go and look at trucks in town. He hadn't said when he'd be back.

Mrs Fyncham had locked the bedroom door when Maria went back down to help her. When she held her ear to the door she thought she could hear her deep breathing, as if she were asleep.

Later that afternoon the phone rang. It rang and rang and Mrs Fyncham didn't stir, so Maria picked up the receiver. She wasn't used to the telephone. There was crackling on the line.

'Hello?'

Nothing.

'Katie?' she didn't know why she said it. Maybe because of the crackling, whoever was there was far away, with perhaps a sea in between them. But the phone clicked and went dead. She put the receiver down. When she turned around she saw Mrs Fyncham standing in the bedroom doorway watching her. She had heard. There was make-up on her face, but she couldn't hide the dark rings under her eyes, and a stain where she had been crying.

'I'll bring you some tea.' Maria turned to go.

Mrs Fyncham took a step towards her. 'You've lived here all your life.'

Maria nodded. It didn't feel safe. There was something pleading in her voice. Maria wanted her to go back into her room. It felt like little hands grappling in the dark towards her and she wanted to brush them away. She didn't want to feel anything for this woman. She didn't belong here.

'How do you do it?' She was still standing there.

'Do what?'

Maria wondered if she should call the doctor. The woman wasn't making sense.

'Live here alone like this, don't you get lonely?' But she didn't wait for a reply; she went back into her room and shut the door.

When Maria took her tea later, she seemed to have recovered. She was lining the bottles of lotion up on her dressing table. It was safe again.

When the sun was on its way down and the shadows were long in the driveway Maria stoked the fire for supper. She had the 'Menu' stuck on the wall. Cooking didn't interest her.

She cut the rhubarb up and let it stew on the stove. Rhubarb and pineapple were poisonous together. They caused a chemical reaction. But there was no pineapple. She was making a pie for Mr Fyncham because he liked it. When she went to close the windows in the sitting room so that the beetles wouldn't fly in she found Mrs Fyncham sitting in an armchair, the bottle of gin next to her on the floor. 'We'll eat on the verandah. You can set the table out there.'

The meal was cold, and still Mr Fyncham hadn't come home. Maria was sent to fetch Mrs Fyncham's cigarettes and another bottle of gin and the magazines. But the light on the stoep was too dim to read by. Mrs Fyncham got up and started pacing around the sitting room. She looked like the wild cat that Maria had found trapped down by her mother's place. It had bitten its own tail off to escape the wire.

She was standing in front of the portrait of Katie when Mr Fyncham came back. Her tongue was like a knife, slicing the air. 'Where were you? I was sick. Where were you?'

'Calm down.' He put his hand out to touch her arm but she lashed out at him, hitting him across the face. He hit her back. She staggered. He put his arms out. This time she let him steady her. 'You shouldn't be drinking.'

'What else am I supposed to do here? There's nothing to do. You have the farming; you're out all day. It's okay for you.'

'Sit down. Come and sit down. I'll get you some water.'

'I don't want water.'

'Will you go to the doctor now?'

She started to cry. She reached for the bottle. He flung it into the bin and it shattered.

'You can't drink.'

'Don't tell me what to do.' She stood up shakily. 'We shouldn't have come here.'

'It was your idea. It's always been your idea.'

'Don't make me feel guilty.'

'What?'

'It's not what I thought. I just can't stay. It's driving me crazy. Nothing to do, just that kaffir girl for company.'

'It's what you wanted, remember.'

'I thought I wanted it.'

'Well *I* want it Isobel.'

'If you didn't go out and leave me. That wasn't part of it.'

'Why don't you go back if you're so unhappy? Leave me here to make the money. It might be better.' He spat the words out and Maria could feel the bitterness. His face had changed, it wasn't the Mr Fyncham she knew that laughed and joked with her.

She pressed herself further back into the shadows in the corner of the room.

'I won't leave you here alone.' Mrs Fyncham was looking at the painting of Katie. 'It's ugly. It's an ugly thing. I want it down. Maria.'

Maria came out from where she had been watching them.

'Take the painting down, take it away.'

Maria looked at Mr Fyncham.

'It's okay, Maria, you can go now.' He was back in control but she could feel the cold air around him.

She had to leave them. She took a candle to her room and lay in bed and stared at the ceiling. All she could hear was their voices shouting. The wind blew in the room – a gust of warm air that extinguished the candle and left her in the dark as the water rushed in. The river swirled around her head.

She saw a woman sitting at a desk, writing. Her hair was pulled back off her face and fastened with a silver clasp, Maria recognised the clasp: she had polished it for Mrs Fyncham.

The woman was bent over the paper, intent on what she was doing, stopping only to fill her pen with ink again. The man behind her was looking away and out of a window into the sunshine outside, mapping and planning. He was unhappy, Maria saw the tension in his shoulders. He knew he shouldn't be there in the room with her.

The woman stopped writing and reached out to touch the man's arm but he wouldn't look at her or what she was doing.

And then Maria saw Katie's face, in the sunlight, smiling at her so clearly that it made her laugh out loud.

The next morning Mr Fyncham had left before sunrise and Mrs Fyncham was up by nine. She looked as though she had slept; she seemed quite cheerful. Maria thought they must have made up. When Maria went to fetch some more toast, she stopped her.

'No, don't go. Sit down here.' She pulled out a chair. 'Mr Fyncham says I should go out more, on the farm, do things.' She laughed as though the idea was ridiculous. 'He says I need to do some exercise. That it will take my mind off …' She stopped and looked at Maria. 'Mr King had a daughter, didn't he? The one in the picture.'

'He had two.'

'Catherine.' She said the name slowly.

'And Lilly, she was the younger.' Maria stepped carefully on loose pebbles. She felt the dark water underneath, the current pulling her.

'Did you play with them?' Her tone was light. She sounded as if she really wasn't very interested, just making conversation.

'With Katie.'

'Where did you play?' Her voice was flat now.

'Up in the koppies, at the river.'

'Do you swim, did you swim in the river?'

'Katie taught me to swim.'

'Mr Fyncham says I should swim. I want you to take me to the place where you swam. You can take me there today.' She stood up and pulled her hair back off her face and tied it with the silver clasp.

'It's hot.' Maria thought she was crazy to go at midday. But she had made up her mind.

'We can take hats.' She snapped. 'You can carry the umbrella.'

Maria was loaded like a packhorse. Mrs Fyncham insisted on taking not just hats and an umbrella but magazines, bottles of cold water, a picnic lunch, and a chair. Gabriel laughed at Maria, hunched over under the weight. He tried to pinch her as she walked past. They had to stop every hundred yards for Mrs Fyncham to rest as she complained of the heat and the grass scratching her. But she wouldn't turn back. Maria's back felt crushed by the time they got down to the pool.

After Mrs Fyncham had changed she made Maria show her a safe place to enter the pool. She swam with her head out of the water. Up and down, breast stroke. Maria sat on the bank, hot and wanting to jump in, but she couldn't – not in the same water, Mrs Fyncham wouldn't have it.

She had to arrange the fold-up chair in the shade so that when Mrs Fyncham came out of the pool she could 'recline' as she put it. Her drink had to be cold and ready. Maria watched her. She had stopped sipping from her glass and was staring up at the ledge above the pool.

'Katie used to jump off there.' Maria didn't know why she said it. She didn't want to talk about Katie to this woman.

'What, off that rock?' Mrs Fyncham sounded scornful. 'I don't think so.'

'She was brave. Her father used to watch her do it.'

Mrs Fyncham looked up quickly.

'Do you ever hear from her, from Katie? Do you think she'll ever come back?'

Maria shook her head. 'No, I haven't heard from her.'

When they had packed up and started back towards the house Mrs Fyncham told Maria to stop and wait, she had forgotten something. She ran back towards the pool. Maria could see her. She hadn't forgotten anything. She was just standing and staring up at the ledge.

Hendrik had watched them from the wattle trees above the pool. He had crouched down so that he wouldn't be spotted. It was the first time he'd seen Mrs Fyncham, although everyone in the district knew that the Fynchams had moved to Hebron. His mother had had the women over for coffee and cakes to discuss it and he had watched them as they had gossiped.

'I've seen Mrs Fyncham in town, nose in the air. Too high and mighty to greet.'

'I saw her in the chemist, buying every cream under the sun. They say she's an *uitlander*.'

'I wonder how long they'll last.'

'They've kept the *mal meid* on. No more lazing around in the yard for her.'

'They've bought the farm you know. Mr King's not coming back. Dead, died of drink. Lost everything.'

'Well that's what comes of adultery.'

'And the daughters?'

'No one's heard. Could be dead for all we know.'

'He's handsome, Mr Fyncham. But don't tell my husband I said so.'

'I don't trust handsome men.'

When Mrs Fyncham and Maria had left, Hendrik walked down to the pool and dived in.

★

Maria went out into the courtyard that night. It was too hot to sleep. She lay down on her back listening to the night sounds, mapping out the star constellations. If she lay for long enough she could leave her body and float up into the warm night until she hovered above the house, high enough to see the roof of the church.

★

The next day Mrs Fyncham went swimming alone. She left Maria plucking a chicken in the kitchen. When she came back her hair was wet and she looked pleased with a secret kind of pleasure.

On the last day of the month Maria and the workers were paid. Mr Fyncham took them all to town to buy supplies. When they got back in the evening Mrs Fyncham had taken the car and gone.

Mr Fyncham said she'd had to go and see a doctor. But after a month she still hadn't returned. He didn't tell Maria anything but every week the phone would ring and he would speak to someone in a hushed tone for a long time, sometimes she heard anger in his voice, sometimes he slammed down the phone. After those calls he would go out in the dark walking. Sometimes he would only come back in the morning.

Mr Fyncham had Maria cook a special meal on payday at the end of the next month. He'd sold cattle and got a good price. He invited her to eat with him. After the meal, he asked her to fetch the chess set.

'Do you play?' he asked her.

She shook her head. She had only read the moves in the chess book.

'I'll teach you.'

She watched as he set the pieces out.

Mrs Fyncham had gone. Maria hadn't seen her, not at night, not on the river, she couldn't even hear her voice anymore. Mr Fyncham didn't talk about her. When the telephone rang he didn't answer it anymore. He didn't want her to come back. He hadn't loved her, Maria knew that. Now he had found another passion besides the farm. He had bought an old plane that he kept near town and he had started to fly. Maria would see him above the farm sometimes, circling up in the blue. Trying to forget.

Maria liked the knights on the chessboard – they were horses. She had galloped with Katie across the veld, sitting behind her on Katie's pony, clinging on, shrieking with fear and joy.

'You are a fast learner,' Mr Fyncham told her. By the end of the evening she had learnt how to play.

The next morning he had put the portrait of Katie back on the wall. Maria thought this meant something.

You think everything means something. She could hear Katie's voice. *Everything is a sign. What does it mean then, the singing in the church?*

Katie was so close now Maria could almost reach out and touch her hand.

Three

It was the weekend – a month after Mrs Fyncham had left Hebron. Hendrik had invited his friend Dirk over to his parents' farm. They had spent the morning searching around the farmhouse and stables for a puffadder that Hendrik's mother had seen in the bushes near the chicken hok. She wanted it taken far away from the house, or shot. Dead was better, she said. But Hendrik hated killing snakes. He would catch them and take them out into the veld. He liked to watch them slide away and hide themselves in the long grass, camouflaged in their surroundings.

After a couple of hours of searching, lifting bushes with their forked sticks and turning over rocks, they gave up and came into the house for lunch. The sun was searing down on the land. The girl had put out cold meats and salad but Hendrik's mother picked at her food.

'Come on Ma, eat something.' Hendrik passed her the plate with sliced ham but she wouldn't. She couldn't; she had no appetite. Her head felt heavy, she was dizzy and needed to lie down for a while. His father was away in town. He'd taken the truck to buy salt lick for the cattle.

Hendrik and Dirk lazed around for a couple of hours listening to the radio. They smoked cigarettes in his room. It was cool inside the house. Then they went to the stables and saddled up two horses. They were going to go down to the part of the river that ran through his farm. The river was full because of the summer rains. Hendrik had made a raft out of ten-gallon drums strapped together. They would see how far they could get down the river before it stormed, maybe all the way to the crossing. The sky was already clouding over.

Dirk rode ahead of Hendrik. He had taken his shotgun and slung it across his back and tightened the leather strap that held it against his back so that it wouldn't bounce when he galloped across the veld.

'In case I see something I want to shoot.' He was trigger-happy. Hendrik hoped that he wouldn't. When Dirk reached the place where the path forked he stopped his horse. Hendrik caught up with him. His horse was impatient to get to the water. Dirk was staring up at the ridge, his eyes were slits in the harsh sun.

'Let's go up there to the church.' He pulled on the reins, drawing his horse's head up from the grass it had been chewing. Then he took the gun off his back and held it with the butt pressed into his shoulder. He stared down the barrel as though he was taking aim, pointing at the church. He pretended to pull the trigger.

'Pow!' He lowered the gun. 'They say the natives worship the devil up there in the kaffir church. They don't believe in God. They pretend, singing the hymns and everything, but up there, there's chicken's blood on the altar. Our kitchen girl said she was walking back that way the other night when she saw a ghost coming out the church. It was white with blood around the mouth. It came running out of the church screaming.'

'And you believe her?' Hendrik pulled his horse's head around and kicked it.

'Come on. I'm hot. Let's go!'

But Dirk was still staring up at the church. 'I'm going up there. We can swim in the pool on the other side.'

'But that's on Hebron. We'd be trespassing.' Hendrik had to get Dirk down to the river, away from the church. He didn't want him to go up there.

'Since when are you frightened of trespassing?' Dirk laughed. He kicked his horse into a canter, heading for the koppie. Hendrik followed him.

When they reached the wattle trees at the bottom, Dirk got off his horse and tied it to a branch of a tree, then started scrambling up the rocks. He jumped from one to another. Hendrik was surprised at how agile he looked for someone so stocky.

'Come on!' he shouted to Hendrik as he leapt from one boulder to the next, going higher and higher up towards the church. Hendrik got off his horse and tied it up to a tree that was in the shade. He moved Dirk's horse from where he had tied it up in the heat of the sun. They could water them when they got to the river.

Dirk had taken off his shirt and was standing with his legs astride on the edge of one of the big granite boulders. He beat his chest and his voice echoed off the rocks. 'Shaka Zulu!' he shouted. Then he took a handful of small stones that he had in his pocket and started hurling them up at the thunderclouds above him. They scattered, bouncing off the rocks down into the krantz below. Hendrik reached him.

'What are you doing – are you crazy?'

'You can't talk. Crazy?' Dirk laughed. 'You're the one who's crazy, Hendrik. You know what they say at school – *different*. That's a polite way of saying fucking crazy.' Hendrik looked away.

'Different. That's what De Beer said. Fucking crazy, I say.' Dirk laughed. 'That's why I like you.' He slapped Hendrik across the back. Then he hurled the last stone up and shouted up to the sky. 'I'm going to make it rain, just you see.' He took his gun and aimed it up at the clouds.

'Stop!' Hendrik yanked the gun out of his hand. They tussled on the rocks. Hendrik was near the edge. The gun slid out of Hendrik's hand down the rocks, and Dirk scrambled down after it.

When they had retrieved it, they lay down on the rocks, exhausted by the heat and the exertion.

'When I leave school I'm going to go and fight the communists in Russia – I'm going to skin a bear and make one of those hats. Drink vodka and fuck those Russian women. Will you come?'

But Hendrik wasn't listening. He had sat up and was staring up at the church. Dirk sat up too.

'What is it?'

Then he saw her too. A woman was standing in the clearing in front of the church. Her back was towards them. She was wearing a yellow dress, the colour of evening primrose; it was blowing up around her legs. Hendrik stared at the pale skin of her thighs. Her hair shone copper and gold in the sunlight.

'Hey!' Dirk shouted and stood up. 'Hey!' But the woman didn't turn around. 'What? Is she deaf or something? Hey what if it's that ghost – I'm going up there.' He picked up the gun but Hendrik had his hand gripped around Dirk's arm. His fingers cut into Dirk's flesh. 'Hey stop it.'

'No.'

'Let's have some fun.'

Hendrik jerked Dirk around so that he faced him. 'What's wrong with you?' Dirk laughed nervously. Hendrik's face was contorted. 'I just want to go closer to see who it is.'

'I know who it is.' Hendrik looked away. Dirk was staring at him, and he didn't want his eyes to give him away or his voice. He looked back towards the farmhouse.

'It's Mrs Fyncham, from Hebron,' he lied as he pulled Dirk down the rocks. They stumbled and slid. There were cuts on their legs when they reached the bottom.

'Hey wait for me.' Dirk shouted as Hendrik got on his horse.

Hendrik turned back once, to see if Dirk was following him. Then he looked up at the church. Catherine was gone.

*

Maria sat next to the pool. She had woken up that morning knowing that something was different, knowing that she had to get down to the river. Katie was coming back; all she had to do was wait.

The air was thick and hot and still; if she had a knife she could slice it apart. The fat black ants were crawling along the rock surface to the pip of the peach she had discarded. They ate the fleshy part quickly and efficiently. She watched them; it was too hot to move. How long did ants live? She would ask Katie when she came. Some people were like ants – always busy. They didn't look up and then they died and they had never seen the sky at night. They had never mapped out the constellations or wondered what was up there. But she and Katie had. By the time they were eight they knew all the stars in the sky.

It was going to storm. The sun was burning the back of her neck – soon she would be as black as those people further up in Africa in the jungle. She ran her hand over her skin. It was still smooth. She laughed at herself. Since Mr Fyncham had come to Hebron she had bought Vaseline with the money he had given her and every day rubbed it into her skin to make it smooth. Her small breasts were still firm, not like her sister who had three children by the time she was eighteen. Her sister's breasts hung like a dog's teats.

Maria had started looking at herself in the mirror again. She had got one of her sisters to braid her hair. The outside of her head was ordered in neat rows. It was a criss-cross of paths; just the inside remained a wilderness. Her head was hot and dazed now; she had waited since the early morning. She bent down and plunged it under the water. When she shook the water off, a rustling sound at the far side of the pool made her turn. She heard someone shouting on the other side of the ridge – boys. She moved back into the bushes in case they came over and down to the pool. But it was silent again. She dangled her feet in the water. The water under the surface was cold. There were insects skidding over the top, walking on water like Jesus in the Bible, only this wasn't classified as a miracle.

And then she looked up and there was Katie standing on the ledge above the pool. Her hair was a golden halo around her pale face. She had appeared so silently that Maria was taken by surprise.

They stared at each other.

Jump, Maria, hold my hand.

I can't swim.

It doesn't matter. I'll help you. I'm counting to three. Come on.

Catherine's yellow dress billowed up like a parachute as she jumped. Then she hit the water and was underneath. Her skin was pale as though she hadn't been in the sun for years. Maria was drenched by the splash she made. The shock made her laugh. Catherine grabbed her ankle under the water and pulled her off the rock into the pool with her. Maria didn't need to pinch herself to see if it was true, she could feel Catherine's grip, firm around her leg. Catherine surfaced. They looked at each other.

'I could have drowned.' Maria spoke first.

'But I knew you could swim. I knew it was you,' Catherine said and she reached out and touched Maria's arm.

Their faces were close together. Everything about Catherine's face was fine – the high cheekbones, her straight nose, the line of her eyebrows. She had the same skew smile and the gap between her teeth was still there. But there was something in her face that showed the strain of the years she had been away. They were years when she had been separated from herself, Maria thought.

Then she lost her footing, slipped on a stone and fell backwards into the water. Catherine held out her hand and pulled her back up towards the rock. They both clambered out and Catherine hugged her. It was a thing to do without thinking. Nobody had hugged Maria for a long time. She didn't know what to say. Catherine didn't know whites didn't do that with natives. It would get her into trouble, Maria thought.

Catherine was standing in the sunlight, the water dripping off her, and Maria knew that she couldn't tell her about the dark things she had seen and felt. About the woman sitting in the shadows at the desk and the man looking out into the light.

'You're wet.' It was all she could think of to say.

'Do you think I'm mad?' Catherine wrung the water out of her dress.

'It should dry quick.' Maria felt the material.

'No, mad to come back.' Catherine sat down. She was feeling in the pocket for something. 'Mad to jump off the rock in my dress. I just wanted to see …' she looked up at the trees and behind them the church. 'I wanted to see if I could still do it. It's high isn't it? But then I haven't jumped off anything for a long time.' She was searching the ground around them. She seemed nervous, Maria thought. All her movements were quick.

'What are you looking for?' Maria asked her.

'Cigarettes. Do you have a cigarette? It's a bad habit, I know. But I really need one.' She bit her lip. 'Can you see how nervous I am. Does it show? What I really need is a drink. I have cigarettes in the car.'

Maria looked at her friend, she couldn't quite believe that she had returned, that she was standing there in front of her asking her for cigarettes as though they had walked there together from the house. As though she'd never been away. She too would be nervous to return, with a strange man in the house and his wife with a tongue like a knife. A wife who had gone but might come back at any time. It was such a big thing to do, to come home after being lost for so long.

'You have a car?' she asked Catherine. And then felt stupid, for how else had she got there, there were no buses.

'I parked it at the store. I couldn't go up to the house. Lilly said I was crazy to come back. You don't think so, do you? I just needed to see for myself.'

'Where is Lilly and your mother?'

'Lilly's in England. Mum's dead.'

'Sorry.' Maria thought of the last time she had seen Mrs King huddled in the back of that black car being driven away, the ashes from where she had burnt her dresses in a pile on the driveway.

'Lilly didn't want me to come back. She said why come back if our father's dead. She said …' Katie put on a funny voice. 'Catherine he didn't leave us anything. Nothing. He was a drunk.' She stared into the water. 'All we have is a letter saying that he died, and his watch. I wasn't sure he was dead. Lilly didn't even want to read the letter. She said she wasn't interested, she had never known him. He hadn't come for us.' Catherine hesitated. 'And then I saw him one night in my sleep. He was standing by this river and I knew he was dead. I also knew he wanted me to come back. He was standing on the riverbank and the angels were singing. It was beautiful.'

A shiver ran through Maria.

'Why don't you lie on the rock – your dress will dry .You can put your head in the shade of the tree.' Maria cleared the rock of sticks so that Catherine could lie down.

'Very sensible.' Catherine looked up and the frown left her face. She had always teased Maria. 'I don't remember you being sensible.'

'You gave me a fright in the pool.'

'Sorry.'

Catherine lay down on the rock and closed her eyes. Maria stared into the water. Catherine had come back. But Mrs Fyncham was out there and Tom was at the house. It wasn't safe.

The sound of a truck on the road made Catherine sit up. She looked up at the wattle trees above the pool and the church. 'Someone put my photograph in the church. Was that you?' she asked Maria.

Maria nodded. They were looking at the trees where they had hidden.

'I did get lost. But you didn't forget about me. You see I remember everything.' Catherine was smiling. That skew charming smile that used to get her out of trouble.

Maria remembered how Catherine smiled even when she was sad. She hid things with that smile.

They were silent for a while. Maria didn't know what to say, she felt tongue-tied but then Catherine spoke.

'So who bought the farm?' She was trying to sound offhand – like it didn't matter.

'Mr Fyncham. He's the new owner.' Maria watched Catherine closely to see if she knew the name, but she could see that she had never heard of him. She wondered what he would do when he saw Katie grown up, come back.

'What's he like?' Part of her wanted to know, part wanted him to remain a faceless stranger who she knew nothing about.

'He's handsome. He's learning how to farm.'

'Just learning?'

'He reads it up in books.' The way Maria said it made them both laugh. Maria stared at her feet as though they didn't belong to her body.

'And my father never came back?' Catherine had said it now. Her fingers were busy plaiting three strands of grass, trying to steady herself.

Maria shook her head. 'He sent managers. I worked for them.' She thought of the hours in the shadows of the house picking up things, stirring pots. 'Mr Fyncham told me that your father died.' She wanted to take Catherine's hand and give it a squeeze. To say she was sorry, but she felt awkward suddenly.

Catherine picked up a pebble and threw it into the water. 'What about you? What happened to you?'

'I stayed here.' Maria took a stick and started drawing in the sand to mask her confusion.

'And your mother?'

'My mother's at home. My sister's looking after her.'

'You don't live there with them?'

Maria shook her head. 'I stay at Hebron. I have a room next to the kitchen.'

'And you didn't marry?'

'No.'

'You never met anyone?'

'I met someone.' She looked up at the church to the graveyard where she had sat on her blanket under the stars to be with him. 'He's buried up there.'

'I'm sorry.'

Maria could see she meant it. Catherine stood up and held out her hand to pull Maria up.

'My dress is nearly dry. Let's go to my car? We can drive up to the house. I can't put it off forever, meeting this Mr Fyncham. I don't even know if he'll let me stay the night.'

Catherine winced as she stood on a rock on the path that led away from the river back to the road. She lifted her foot and examined it. 'All soft and pale,' she said disparagingly. 'I left my shoes in the car. I thought my feet were tougher than they are.'

When they got near the road Catherine stopped. She looked at Maria as though she was trying to work something out. 'Do you still see things?' she asked her.

Maria nodded.

'Did you see me?'

'Sometimes. One or two times.'

'Where was I?'

'On the beach.'

'We lived by the sea in England, in a place called Salcombe, Mum and Lilly and me.' Catherine hesitated, then she shook her head as if to shake off a thought. 'Did you see anything else?'

Maria shook her head.

'Is this Mr Fyncham married?'

'His wife she went away. I don't think she's coming back. She drank a lot.'

'Like me.'

Maria looked up.

'I'm sober now. Watch.' Catherine hopped on one leg down the path in front of Maria. 'So she just left one day? Didn't say where she was going, when she'd be back?'

'He doesn't speak about her.'

'Perhaps he's got her locked in the cellar.'

'No, I looked.'

Catherine laughed. 'I wasn't serious. Do you think he'll let me stay?'

They had reached the road and the school building. The school children crowded around Catherine's car. They had written in the dust on the window: *I need kleen*. They wanted to touch her skin. She held out her arm and they ran their fingers along the fine golden hairs. Maria clapped her hands and slapped at them, but Catherine stopped her. 'I like it,' she said.

Catherine opened the car door and Maria sat down carefully on the leather seat as though it might break. It was the first time she had been in a car. When they went down to the store for supplies they went on the trucks or on the trailer behind the tractor.

The floor of the car was strewn with empty cooldrink bottles, cigarette packets, maps and books. There was dust everywhere.

Catherine leant across and felt in the cubbyhole for her cigarettes. She handed them to Maria. 'Won't you light me one?'

That was the part that Maria had loved when they had stolen Mr King's cigarettes. It had made them feel so grown-up even though they had choked on it.

'Springboks.' Maria lit the cigarette and inhaled. 'Cowboy cigarettes.' She coughed.

'I got them at the railway siding.'

They had reached the gate and Catherine sped up as she rounded the corner into the driveway. 'You'll kill us!' Maria protested, but she was laughing at the same time.

'Do you like my car?' Catherine skidded to a halt in front of the house.

'Where did you get it?'

'Johannesburg. I saw Mrs Coombe there. Do you remember her? I stayed with her.'

'With Mrs Coombe, but …' Maria thought of Katie riding with her teaspoon across the grass towards something she couldn't stop.

'I know. It's hard to believe but she was the only person whose name I knew when I got here and I looked up her address.'

★

Mrs Coombe was not the woman that Catherine had remembered; the cold, distant woman with the china skin who had stolen her father. This woman lived in a house in the white suburbs. Natives were being moved out of town – they needed a pass to come to work now, Mrs Coombe had told Catherine, it was the way things were. It was separate development – the new apartheid policy – it would be better this way, she explained.

Catherine thought of Maria. She would show them on the farm that not all whites believed in this new policy. She thought of her own separate development in a foreign country, separated from everything that had been her world.

There was no noise in the streets. A man walked his terrier along the pavement. Two maids sat out on the grass verge talking – when it got dark they would have to go back to the townships to their own children. A woman in a driveway watched her husband watching the gardener washing the car.

Mrs Coombe's house was dark inside and frousty. It smelled of cabbage and mothballs. But Mrs Coombe had sweetness about her, a self-effacing tentativeness that Catherine had never seen.

She had made a bed up for Catherine and turned down the cover. There was a jug of water with a rose in it on the bedside table.

Catherine had waited in the sitting room while Mrs Coombe arranged the tea. The room was full of knick-knacks: china dogs, vases, a serviette holder fashioned into a Spanish woman that held serviettes in her skirt. She walked around looking at the things that Mrs Coombe had collected over the years. She stopped in front of a framed collage on the wall. It was made from postcards that had been stuck together. She ran her finger over the glass. It was so different from anything else in the room. It came from another place; another life somewhere in a tropical place with palm trees and a turquoise sea and black fishermen. In the centre was a fortress, an old crumbling building that had been grand once, with a palm tree growing in the ruins and steps leading down into the water. The cards had faded with age.

Mrs Coombe came in with the tea tray. Catherine took a sugar biscuit in the shape of a heart from the tin. Mrs Coombe looked up at the postcards. 'From a friend.' She flushed. Then she turned to Catherine. 'I'm afraid my life hasn't been very exciting,' she said quietly.

*

'Your cigarette.' Maria put her hand out to catch the ash that was about to fall on Catherine's dress. They had been sitting in the car for a while. Catherine handed Maria the rest of her cigarette. 'You finish it. I'm too nervous.'

Catherine got out of the car. Maria noticed that she had left her shoes behind and that she was walking up the stairs barefoot. She got out the car and called to Catherine, but it was too late, the huge arched door had opened and Mr Fyncham was standing there waiting.

Four

Tom Fyncham had let her stay in her old room in her old wooden bed with the loose slats. Maria had given her a cotton sheet; it was too hot for blankets. Catherine could hear Mr Fyncham moving in the next room, in her parents' bedroom. If he had felt uncomfortable about her being there he hadn't shown it. He had been polite and charming over dinner; and at the end she realised that he hadn't told her anything about himself. He had asked her a lot of things and she had said too much, and he had talked about the farm. She had seen how proud he was of all the things he had done, and that he loved it. And he was handsome, Maria was right.

Are you attracted to him? She could hear Lilly's voice as though to be attracted was something unsavoury – like dirty underwear, to be held between your fingers at a distance. But to Catherine it felt like electric currents in the air that made one's hair stand on end and that gave you shocks in your fingertips.

He hadn't talked about his wife and he had made it clear without saying anything that she couldn't ask him. She thought of him folding his clothes. He wouldn't throw them on the floor like she did; he was too controlled for that. But he was not obsessive, not like Hesketh in England. 'Call me Tom,' he had said.

Tom Fyncham would put his clothes back in the wardrobe where they had come from. But not her, he wouldn't want to put her back, not where she belonged anyway. It was his house.

All she wanted was to be allowed to stay for a few days in the house, to ride in the veld, to go up to the tin church with Maria and then to say goodbye.

The paint was peeling off the walls and there were cobwebs in the corners where Maria's brush hadn't reached or she hadn't bothered to clean.

'Your house is my house,' he had said, so graciously. But then he had laughed at himself and she had felt relieved, it had sounded too grand. She couldn't stay – not if his wife was coming back.

There was one thing that was different about the room. Someone had taken Lilly's bed out. She could hear her sister's voice as she lay, staring at watermarks on the ceiling. She could see Lilly standing in their house in Salcombe with her hands on her hips. And Hesketh, a shadow in the background watching them.

'Why do you want to go back? There's nothing there. It's not going to bring him back, you know. He's dead, Catherine.'

'I know that. Don't you think …'

'He didn't come for us. He didn't even write. He drank himself to death. All they sent was his watch.'

'Shut up, Lilly. Just shut up.' She could have hit her then, battered her head against the wall.

'Who are you going back to? Who are you hoping to find?'

'Maria's there.'

'She's a servant. It's not the same. You're not girls anymore. You're grown-up. You can't stay eight forever you know. You have to move on Catherine. Besides, people won't understand there. Blacks are servants, they can't be your friends.'

'Really, fancy that! I could have sworn.'

'Oh, don't fool around, Catherine! Be serious for once. Why do you always have to make a joke of things that are serious?'

For protection. They had learnt that when they were little, she and Maria. You laughed for protection. You joked and things were not so bad.

'You don't know how serious I am.'

'What are you going to do there? Well?'

'It doesn't matter.' She was tired. 'Just go away, Lilly.'

'Have you been drinking?'

'No, have you?'

'Why do you have to drink so much?'

'Because I feel trapped here.'

'Why can't you just have one glass? You think of no one but yourself. What about Hesketh? How does he feel? We can't always have what we want. We can't have everything.' On and on like a stuck record.

'Why not?'

'Oh, come on.'

'Do you think I don't know that? Who nursed Mum when she was dying? Who mopped up her vomit? Not you, Lilly, you were too squeamish. There are no rules for how we should live.'

'Hesketh is good for you. Mother and I ...'

'Leave Mum out of this. How do you know what's good for me? You don't even know what's good for yourself.'

But Lilly wasn't listening.

'We thought if you had children ...'

'What? What did you think? That it would grow me up?'

'What do you want?'

I want what Mr Fyncham has. I want to stay here. I want to farm and paint and belong. She spread her fingers in the dark. Is that too much?

She got out of bed and pushed the window up and leant out. The sky was lit up with streaks of lightning and there was the rumble of thunder far away. She closed her eyes and smelled the rain coming. There would be a storm. The clouds would slash open and the rain would hit the dry earth and release the acrid smell and she would be able to breathe again. In England the rain had been different.

'Where are you going, Catherine? It's late.'

'Out, Lilly. I'm going out. You can't stop me.'

'But it's raining.'

'I need to get out of here.'

'You must calm down. Are you panicking?'

'What does it look like?'

'Tell me about it.' Hesketh's soothing suffocating voice as he sat in the corner. 'Tell me what makes you panic, what are you feeling?'

'You – you, you, you make me panic.' But she can't say it – it sticks in her throat.

'It's okay, Catherine, I'm here for you.'

She runs out onto the beach, leaving them to talk behind her back. The birds skitter across the sand in front of her. Their legs are a whir of movement. She is trying to run out of herself. They don't know that. They are sitting in the lamplight. Lilly is leaning forward. Hesketh rests his hand on her knee. Lilly sighs.

'Catherine has no control. She has no sense of what is appropriate to say and do and what is not. She's a woman now, she can't behave …' They are drinking tea together. Sip, sip, swish it round their mouths, and swallow. 'It's getting worse. I don't know why she does these mad things. When she comes back she will be soaked, you know.'

Her mother had understood. She had wanted to feel the rain too. Before she died she had asked Catherine to open the window so that she could stick her arms out into the cold night and feel the water against her skin.

A streak of lightning lit up the church. Catherine saw it from her window and wondered if Maria was up there. She remembered the word for rain in Swazi. Other words too. They would all come back. It was meant to be like riding a bicycle. Words floating in the air: dog, cat, horse, run, mother, swim, river, father. She said them under her breath. If she could say them she could stay. But she couldn't join them together; they were like the beetles flying in the dark, unconnected, buzzing around.

She would need another drink to make her sleep, and perhaps something stronger. The passage was dark and she left the door to her room open so that she could see as she walked to the sitting room. Mr Fyncham's door was closed and there was no noise in the house. He had left a bottle of whisky on the piano – perhaps he had known that she would need it, perhaps he was expecting her. The lamp shed a circle of light on the carpet. He had left the front door open, or Maria had forgotten to close it. Catherine took the whisky bottle out onto the stoep. There was a rumble of thunder and a door banged shut somewhere in the house.

In the morning she would ask Tom Fyncham if she could borrow a horse and go riding to the boundaries of the farm and down to the river.

In the winter they burnt the grass on the farm. Maria and she had run over the blackened stubble, testing themselves to see who was chicken.

The noises in her head had become like background static; like a radio. She listened to the thunder and to her heart beating and she closed her eyes and smelt the wild smell of plants in the garden and the scent of the lilies. She lay down on the wall of the stoep and watched the stars. They had known about those constellations.

'Maria. Look up there.'

'What?'

'There's animals up there in the stars. Bulls, cows, sheep.'

'What kind of sheep? Dorpers or merinos?'

'I don't know.'

'Have they got big horns?'

'No.'

'Then they're dorpers. Are there chickens up there?'

'What?'

'Up there, are there chickens?'

'You're crazy?'

'Chickens in the sky. I think there's a chicken man up there. He keep a chicken under his arm and it lay the stars.'

'You're crazy.'

It started to rain; big drops pelted the roof. The window to her parents' room was open and banging. Things inside the room, near the window, would be getting soaked. Tom Fyncham couldn't be in there or he would have shut the window. He must have gone out, but she hadn't heard him.

She went down the steps and out onto the driveway and stood in the rain. She could stand there until she was soaked, it was like swimming and then you could get dry afterwards. She didn't know how long she had stood there or how long he had been standing next to her when he spoke.

'Do you often stand in the rain?' He was right beside her but she couldn't see his face clearly in the dark.

'Do you often go out walking at night in a storm?' She surprised herself by her quick retort. But he didn't answer her.

'Is something wrong? Has something happened?' She could see his face now. She could feel him standing so close to her.

'No,' he shook his head 'I just couldn't sleep.'

She couldn't think of what to say to him, the words were stuck somewhere, but she wanted to reach out and take his hand, it was so close – Lilly would say that was inappropriate behaviour. 'You can't just do what you feel all the time. Where would the world be?' But he stepped away from her. 'I'm going inside. I need something hot to drink. You're welcome to join me.'

'I'll come in soon.'

She watched him run up the steps out of the rain.

She was getting cold too now.

When she got inside he had changed his clothes and made them some coffee. He brought her a towel and they sat out on the stoep together. The downpour had stopped as quickly as it had started.

'If it's hot sometimes I sleep out here.' He was watching her, and she looked away, up to the church. There was a light burning. 'Someone's up there, in the church.'

'You've been there?' She turned to him.

'You sound surprised. It's on my land.' He had taken a packet of cigarettes and lit one. 'Do you want one?'

She struggled to light the match. He leant across and cupped his hands around hers so that she could light it, it made her skin shiver.

'It must be strange for you, to come back and find someone else here in your house.'

He was doing it again, finding out more about her than she of him. She would have to be guarded, she shouldn't just trust him like that, although she felt she could tell him anything without it mattering, without Lilly's disapproval, or Hesketh's analysis. In some strange way she thought this stranger knew her better already than they had ever done.

'Did you meet him, my father, when you bought the farm?'

All she could see clearly was the glow of his cigarette.

'No.' He shook his head. He threw the cigarette down and crushed it under his foot. He had only smoked half of it. 'Catherine, there's something …' He was standing in front of her, looking at her. But he changed his mind about what he was going to say. 'I'm tired. I'm going to bed. I'm getting up early to go flying.'

'You have a plane?'

'Is that not allowed?' He was teasing her now.

'Where is it? Do you keep it here? I didn't see it.'

'There's a small landing strip outside town. Why don't you join me tomorrow?'

'Did you fly in the war?' She hadn't answered him. She wanted to stall this next step.

'Yes.' He was standing waiting for her to go inside with him.

'Where?'

'All over. I'm leaving early.' He opened the door.

She hesitated. Part of her wanted to stay out in the dark; to walk through the trees up to the church to see who had left the light burning.

'Does your wife fly?' Now she had said the wrong thing.

'No. Isobel never came flying.'

'When is she coming back?' It was out there, between them. She couldn't take it back but she wanted to stuff the words back in her mouth and swallow them. Lilly was right, that was inappropriate, and too soon, and she didn't want to know.

'I don't know. I don't think she will.' He was inside now, walking away from her. She followed him down the passage. At the door to his bedroom he turned to look at her. 'I'm leaving early if you want to come. I hope you sleep well.' He was gone.

In her room she took off her nightgown and hung it over a chair to dry and then got into bed, pulling the sheet up around her. He must have still been awake because she could hear the floorboards creak once or twice. So he flew.

The house breathed at night, as though it had a life of its own. The wood expanded and contracted, the wind sighed down the passages. The rain drummed on the tin roof. She thought of Maria searching the cellar for a body. She thought of the light in the church.

She let herself go down, further and further, breathing slower and deeper like a diver descending through the water to a place of stillness, breath and bubbles and colours, a film without sound.

'Katie!'

'I'm coming.'

'Hurry.' Maria's voice is urgent. 'We'll be late.'

'I'm coming. Wait.' She looks down. She is standing ankle deep in water. It is warm and the sun shines on her face. She feels light. Maria is running ahead of her across the sand. Maria stops and turns back, calling into the wind.

She tries to run after her but her legs are stuck. A cloud blocks the sun and it turns cold suddenly. Her legs are slowly sinking in the sand under the water; there is kelp wrapped around her ankles. She can't hear Maria's voice anymore and when she looks up her friend is gone – there is someone else standing on the shore ahead of her – she can't see clearly. But it's a girl with dark hair. She stands and stares.

★

Maria was still up. She had watched Tom and Catherine talking together over supper and she had felt alone, eating by herself in the kitchen. They had talked and laughed and he had told Catherine about places he had been that Maria had only read about in books. When she had come to take the dishes away Catherine had stood up and stacked them herself and gone with her into the kitchen, but then she had returned to Mr Fyncham, it would have been impolite to stay talking in the kitchen. But Maria knew also that Catherine liked the new owner of Hebron, she wanted to talk more, she wanted to find out. There was electricity outside in the thunderclouds and inside the house now too.

Catherine was asleep now. Maria went to the cupboard in the sitting room and took out her container that she kept her beads in. She sat down, threaded a needle and then started to pick up the beads with the tip of the needle: gold, green, black and red for blood. They slid down the cotton making patterns. It stilled her hands and her head. She could tell Catherine things she had seen at the farm, she could tell her about the managers and the things she had read. And she would take her into the veld and pick mushrooms and plait her hair. She had let too much rush out at once; all the sand in her hands. She had spread her fingers and let it all pour out. She should have let it trickle out slowly. There had to be something held back. In the books there was a word, 'enigmatic' – it kept people there. Mr Fyncham was enigmatic. He would keep his secret from Catherine and so would Maria, and if Mrs Fyncham came back Maria could take Catherine to the tin church. They would be safe there.

Five

It was still very early; the sky was pale blue and the air was cool. The clouds had cleared from the night before. It was going to be a hot day. Someone was knocking on Catherine's door, but by the time she had got out of bed and gone into the passage they had gone. She found a cup of tea waiting for her by the door.

When she had dressed she went through to the kitchen to find Maria and thank her. She had remembered just how she liked her tea, really sweet and milky. But Maria wasn't in the kitchen and when Catherine knocked lightly on her door there was no answer. There was no sign of her in the house. She went outside to look in the yard and found Tom working on his car in the driveway. She watched him for a while thinking that he hadn't realised she was there, he was so absorbed in what he was doing. But when he did look up, she realised he had known that she was there all the time. 'So you're coming.' It wasn't a question.

'How long will it take?' It was dangerous. To agree to go flying would be another step away from herself and towards him and then she might lose her footing and slide without being able to stop.

'You don't have to come.'

What if Maria woke up and found them gone? The thought raced through her head.

'You can leave her a note,' he said, as if he'd read her thoughts.

'I know that.'

'Of course you do.'

He was teasing her again.

'I'll get my things.' She went back into the house.

He called after her, 'Bring something warm.'

She wrote Maria a note and left it on the piano. Then she walked down the steps to join him next to the car. He was bent over the engine – his hands greasy with engine oil. She could sense he was pleased.

'Won't you get in and see if she starts. I'll tell you when.'

The inside of the car was clean and polished, not like hers. She looked in the cubbyhole. *Fiddle fingers*, Lilly called her. *You can never leave anything where it's supposed to be. It will get you into trouble.* There was a map. Quickly she unfolded it and just had time to see the red circles and crosses marked at different places, and a coastline on it when he called out.

'Okay, now.'

She turned the key. The engine started with a splutter.

'Okay.' He closed the bonnet and came around to the driver's side. 'Hop over. We're ready to go now.' He was wiping the oil off his hands. She noticed a long scar that stretched from his thumb down across his wrist and wondered what he had done to himself or someone had done to him. Perhaps it was an accident, he had fallen from a horse or cut it on some wire.

'You know a lot about cars.' She felt awkward with him in the daylight. It wasn't so easy to talk.

As they drove up the hill he hummed a tune. It was only when they got to the tar road into town that he turned to look at her.

'Did you sleep well?' he asked.

'Yes, after all the whisky. You?'

'I don't sleep well.' He said it matter of factly.

She didn't know why she had agreed to go flying. She had come to see Maria, to see the house. Now he would take her flying over the farm and she would want to do it again and again. Hesketh said that she had an addictive personality. If there were limits she could never find them.

The opposite was true of this man, she thought. He was engaging but at the same time there were boundaries and border posts with passport controls and sniffer dogs. He was self-sufficient. He wouldn't let her in, not easily.

'What is it?' He was looking at her and she realised she had said 'borders' out loud.

'Nothing. I was just thinking.'

'As one does.'

'As one does.'

'You're going to like this.'

'How do you know?' But she wasn't angry that he presumed. He loved flying, Catherine could see that. And he was charming, Maria was right. His energy was contagious. She opened the window and put her arm out to feel the wind.

'It's further into town than I remembered.' She thought he hadn't heard her because he didn't reply, he was humming that tune again. But then he turned and looked at her as though he was trying to uncover something.

'So, you left your sister back in England?'

'I didn't leave her.' She was relieved that he was concentrating on the road again, it had been unnerving, him looking at her like that.

'But she's still there with your mother.'

'My mother died.'

'I didn't know, I'm sorry.' He sounded surprised, as though he should have known.

'That's why I came back. She left some money; I wanted to come back to say goodbye. There was nothing to keep me there.'

'No man?'

She didn't answer.

'I am sorry about your father.' He was adjusting his side mirror. She couldn't see his face.

'Perhaps I shouldn't have come back.'

He ignored this.

'Do you like jazz?' He was finding a station on the radio. His fingers started to drum a rhythm out on the steering wheel. 'So, do you like jazz?'

'I like to dance.'

'I'll have to take you dancing then.'

They were on the outskirts of town.

★

Maria woke up to a silent house. She would make Catherine a special breakfast. They would sit out in the courtyard and she would tell Catherine about her life and Catherine would tell her what had happened to her in England. She would tell her what she was going to do now and what she thought of Mr Fyncham. She went out onto the driveway and bent down to pick up a hair clip that had fallen. Catherine must have dropped it when she arrived. The hens had made a nest in the bushes on the edge of the vegetable garden and she put her hand in and felt the eggs. They were still warm. She carried them in her skirt. She picked some spinach and some flowers, chrysanthemums, she loved the smell of them, and buried her face in their petals. Mrs Fyncham had gone. No more breakfast trays sent back to the kitchen because the eggs were cold. No more cleaning red lipstick off glasses. She began to remember what she had dreamed.

She had been chasing Katie down the path to the pool. There was movement in the reeds at the side of the water. Mrs Fyncham had been watching them as they ran down the path. Maria called to Katie to stop, but she hadn't heard. When she looked again at the reeds Mrs Fyncham had gone – she had been sucked down into the mud or lifted up into the air – disappeared. That's what they all wanted, for her to disappear.

In the kitchen Maria cracked the eggs into the frying pan, then cut bread and put it in the grid to toast on the stove. Coffee, eggs, toast, juice. She would tell Catherine about the boys she had kissed in the cellar and the Italian prisoners of war and the managers that came and went at Hebron. All these things she had buried, covered with a layer of red dust, but she could still make out the shapes. Now she could blow the dust off and look at them again.

She put the breakfast things on a tray and took them out to where she had set a table with two places.

It was nine o'clock. Catherine had slept long enough. But when Maria knocked on the door there was no answer, and when she opened the door she found that Catherine had gone. They must have left together. Mr Fyncham had taken her flying.

Maria sat and tried to eat breakfast, but she had lost her appetite.

For a while she sat out on the stoep staring down the driveway, then she went inside to wait. She watched the hands of the grandfather clock. The ticking slurred in her head. Images slid in and out.

*

Tom pulled into a garage to fill up with petrol. An elderly white man in an overall walked slowly over towards the car. Tom got out to greet him. Tom was obviously a regular at the garage, Catherine thought. He must have said something about her because the man came around to her window and bent down to look in at her.

'Catherine King.' He held out his hand. 'Mr King's girl. Don't you remember me?'

His hand was sweaty, and Catherine resisted the impulse to wipe her hand after she had shaken his. 'You used to come and get paraffin when I was down at the railway siding. You and your picannin friend, always together.' He laughed, it was a harsh, rasping sound. 'I thought you were a boy the first time I saw you. You and that little picannin. Let me look at you; so you've come back.'

'I'm just visiting.' Catherine looked around for Tom, but he had gone to fetch a can of oil from inside the garage building.

'The last time I saw your father …' He scratched his head. 'It was before the war. He drove out of here and never came back. Ag, it was a shame.' He shook his head. Catherine remembered the man now. He was the man who had beaten one of his workers half to death for filling someone's tank up with diesel instead of petrol.

'So how she's running?' The man turned to Tom as he came back.

He ran his hand over the bonnet. 'You can tell this car's from the coast. You want to watch these spots of rust. Keep the car up here on the highveld, they'll be no problem.'

Tom filled up a container in the boot with petrol.

Catherine turned around to look back as they drove away from the garage. The man was standing waving.

⋆

At lunchtime Maria left the house and started out for the river. When she got near the pool she heard the sound of the aeroplane above her and squinted up at the giant insect. They were up there together. She was a tiny pinpoint – an ant on the ground. She waved up at the sky and the plane turned and circled over the church.

⋆

Catherine looked down and saw the tin church from above. She saw, for the first time, that a large white cross was painted on the roof. Tom turned the plane and flew down over Hebron.

He was turning back, circling. She wanted to bring Maria up here. She wanted to learn to fly herself so that she didn't need anyone to take her up. He had been right, somehow he had known – she had always loved flying. Even from the ground.

'What are you doing?'

'I'm watching the planes, Lilly.'

She lies on her back in the dunes, in amongst the tufts of grass, watching the planes flying over.

'War – I love it,' she whispers.

'Come inside, it's not safe, the bombs.'

'I'd rather risk a bomb than be stuck inside with you,' she thinks. 'The war's the best thing that's happened to me since I left the farm. It's the best thing!' She shouts into the wind.

'How can you speak like that Catherine?'

'It's the truth. It makes me feel alive. I'm going to learn to fly. I want to be up there. I want to disappear.'

She looked down at the land again and this time saw two riders galloping across the veld. They circled the church once more. They were over the river pool now and looking down, she could make out a figure standing in the reeds at the water's edge.

For a moment she thought it was Mrs Fyncham, standing there staring up at the aeroplane, unaware that Catherine was up there with her husband. Catherine felt cold; Mrs Fyncham had come back to Hebron. She would be at the house waiting for her husband when they got home.

But then the figure moved out into the sunshine and Catherine recognised the orange of Maria's skirt.

★

When they got back to Hebron, Tom went down to the stables and Catherine looked for Maria. She wanted to tell her the good news – that Tom had said she could stay at Hebron as long as she wanted. She could help in the farm school. She would learn to fly and take Maria up and show her the top of the church. But Maria wasn't in the house.

When Tom came back he took her into the room that her mother had used for lessons. It had been cleaned out of furniture, apart from a desk and shelves along the wall.

'You could paint in here. The light's good.' He opened the windows.

'This room still smells of bees.' She bent down and smelled the wood of the shelves. 'Did you know that there's a hive under the floorboards.'

'No. There's a lot I don't know. I'll have to get Maria to clean in here. She's useless at cleaning, you know. She reads all day. She's read most of the books on the shelves.'

'I taught her to read. I taught her how to speak English like that too.'

'So it's your fault.'

'What?'

'That she can't fit in.'

'What do you mean?'

'Just that.'

Catherine turned away from him. What did he know? He was distracted, looking out down the driveway. He knew nothing. He didn't understand.

'We used to have lessons in here.' She ran her hand over the desk, collecting dust on her fingers.

'And what did you learn?' He was still looking out of the window. His tone had changed, the lightness had gone quite suddenly. She couldn't tell from his voice if he was genuinely interested, or mocking her.

'All kinds of things.' She turned back to look at him. 'How to behave.'

'So, you didn't learn anything.' It was okay, he was laughing. With him it was like clouds moving over the sun, cold for a second, but then reassuringly warm again and then another cloud came. 'Sometimes it's better not to know the truth. There's no going back then. You can just go forward.'

'I don't think so, not in the end.'

When he spoke again it was abrupt. 'The boys are waiting, I have to go. I'll be back later.'

She watched him from the window as he walked away from the house. She thought he would turn and look back to see if she was watching him. But he didn't. She traced her finger over the letters they had carved in the desk with a penknife. Her father had given it to her for her eighth birthday.

'Write your name, Maria.'

'I can't write.'

'What do you mean? Everyone can write. Here, I'll show you.'

'Not with a knife. Not on the table.'

'I'll take the blame.'

'Now you try. Try with the chalk on the slate. Write: Maria loves Philemon. She wants to kiss him in the stable and have his babies.'

'No.'

'Go on, write it.'

She had lost the knife on one of their journeys along the river. The light was fading now and Maria still hadn't come home. Catherine went to the kitchen and got a tin of polish and a rag. She got down on her knees in the room that was to be her painting room and started to polish – round and round – until the wood began to shine. He would say it wasn't her job to clean – it was Maria's.

She shouldn't trust him to let her stay. She shouldn't let herself be taken in. He would want her to leave. When he came back he would have changed his mind.

But when he came back late in the afternoon, he was singing, one of the jazz tunes that she had heard on the radio.

He had torn a piece of his shirt off and wrapped it around his hand, which he'd cut on some barbed wire when they were fencing down in the camp by the old store. The blood was seeping through. She asked him if he shouldn't have stitches and offered to drive him into town. 'It's not as bad as it looks. I've had worse. I used to fight for a living.' He was joking, but it took her a second. 'What I would like is a cigarette. I've run out.'

She went to fetch her packet in the bedroom. When she came back he'd put a record on and was mixing drinks. He stopped what he was doing and smiled at her, and his whole face relaxed. 'I love it here. I didn't know I would, but I do. I wouldn't want to do anything else now.'

She took a lemon from his pile and began to slice it, concentrating on getting the slices as thin as she could – concentrating on her breathing.

'I'll teach you how to make a daiquiri.' He took the slices of lemon from her.

She began to relax. 'I suppose you worked in a bar too? Prize fighter, bartender?'

'Worked in a bar, excavated for gold, charted unknown territories, wrestled with crocodiles.'

He wasn't going to give anything away.

He added the slices of lemon to the drinks, and ice.

'No umbrellas, I'm afraid.'

'We'll pretend, shall we?'

'Looks like we'll be making our own dinner tonight. Can you cook?'

'Maria will come back before it's dark.' But Catherine didn't feel so certain. She was getting worried. She hadn't seen Maria all day.

'You seem very sure. But then I forget that you've known each other for so long.' There was an edge to his voice, that gentle mocking that confused her.

'People change.'

'Have you changed?' It was a challenge.

She looked straight into his eyes. 'No, not really. I still think I want the same things.'

'So what do you want?' He stirred his drink with his finger. He was flirting with her, she knew, and she was enjoying it. She couldn't help it.

She looked away. He knew what she wanted – it was what he had.

When she looked at him she expected to see triumph or smugness on his face – instead she saw something else. It was the same expression that she had seen on her father's face when she'd asked him if Maria could come and live in the house with them, and he had said no and couldn't give her a reason.

'I'm starving.' She stood up. It was getting too intense. She wasn't good at intensity – it made her panic.

'That's easy.' He seemed relieved that she had changed the subject. 'I'll whip up a beef stroganoff and meringues for pudding.'

'A chef as well?'

He laughed.

★

Walking down the hill from the church, along the path to Hebron, in the evening light Maria sang to herself. A silly clapping song.

Down by the bramble bushes
Down by the sea
Boom boom boom
True love for you my darling
True love for me
When we get married
We'll have a family
And we'll live happily.
Say say my playmate
Come play with me …

She had never been to the sea. Katie had.

'Is she still so pretty?' Maria's mother had asked her. 'What a beautiful girl. What lovely hair.'

'White hair, Mama, you always say that. You think the woman in the store has nice hair, just because it's long and straight. It's always oily, you can fry an egg on it.'

'But Katie has lovely hair.'

'Yes.'

'I used to brush it. You must bring her down to visit me. Promise me. Is she married? It's time you got married. You're going to be too old. Nobody will want you.'

She had her books. She had the ice at the south and north poles and the jungles in between. But when she had tried to read that afternoon, in the quiet of the church, all she could think of was Catherine and Tom. She had wanted Catherine to come back, but now she felt lost. She hadn't seen them all day.

When she reached the gate to Hebron, Maria saw Catherine and Tom sitting on the stoep in a bubble of light, and she held back in the shadows. They were eating supper together. Tom went into the house, and Catherine stood up. She was looking up at the ridge. Maria knew that she was looking to see if there was a light burning in the church, if there was anyone up there in the dark.

'What are you going to paint? Now that you've got a room to paint in.' Tom had come back with coffee.

'I don't know. The river. Maria, if she'll sit still.'

'She told me that you play the piano.'

'What else did she tell you?'

The moon had come into view above the ridge.

Did she tell you what we did in the church? That we made a wish.

But Tom didn't answer. Maria had come out of the shadows into the light.

'Well, look who's here.' There was a hint of sarcasm in Tom's voice that Catherine didn't like.

'My mother was ill.' Maria didn't look at Catherine.

'She doesn't have to make excuses.' Catherine stood up and moved to where Maria was standing by the door. 'There's food left over. I'll heat it up.'

'I'm sure she can do that,' Tom said.

'We're finished anyway. I'll come with you, Maria.' Catherine followed her through to the kitchen.

'Your mother, is she very sick?' Catherine asked as she dished Maria some meat and potatoes.

'She has TB. Some days she feels worse than others. She asked after you.'

'Will you take me down to see her? We'll go together.'

'Yes.'

Catherine sat on the table. There was awkwardness between them. Maria didn't want to talk.

'I'm sorry I didn't see you today. We left early. He took me flying. I'm going to stay here. Tom, Mr Fyncham asked me to help in the school, I can stay in the house.'

'What about …'

'I don't know. She's gone. The important thing is I can stay.' Catherine reached for the bottle of wine they had been drinking at supper. 'Here, let's have some, to celebrate.' She poured them each a glass.

'I'll have to do some things with him if I stay. Like today. I'm going to learn to fly – I'll take you up there with me as soon as I can. Did you know there's a cross painted on the roof of the church?'

Maria shook her head.

'I saw you walking by the pool.' Maria looked up when Catherine said this.

'I saw you too. The plane sounded like an insect up there in the sky.'

'Do you remember when we caught that grasshopper and made Lilly scream?'

She had made Maria smile again.

When Catherine went back out Tom had gone to his room. What did he do in there? Read? Look at his maps? Write? He wasn't going to tell her. She lay in bed, listening. She thought about good things. About Maria and what they had done together and it made her feel safe.

Christmas beetles. If you catch them you can make them sing by squeezing them.

It's so quiet in the house; it makes the outside noises loud. I can hear the mice in the roof playing football. Up and down they scurry. One goal, two goals. Dancing: one two cha, cha, cha. Do you like jazz? Do you want to learn to fly? What do you want?

My fingers are pale in the dark.

'Maria, stop wriggling.'

'Mama doesn't know I'm here. She think I'm asleep in the pondok.'

'Why do you call it a pondok?'

'It is a pondok. There's no proper beds and no water in taps.'

'Lie still.'

'What if your mother come to see you in the night? Katie, do you hear me?'

'She won't. She takes pills to make her sleep. Tomorrow, let's go up to the church at night.'

'Why?'

'You know why.'

'I can't sleep.'

'Count sheep – it'll help you to fall asleep.'

'Dorpers or merinos?'

'Why do you always ask that? Does it matter, Maria?'

'What if they go backwards? What if they start going too fast? Sleep, sheep sleep sheep sheep sleep …'

Catherine got up and walked to the sitting room. There was a new whisky bottle on the shelf. She wondered if he'd left it out for her, if he had gone out at night and was planning to come back and talk to her. But when she went out it wasn't him sitting on the wall of the stoep reading with a torch, it was Maria.

Catherine looked over her shoulder. 'The book is upside down,' she pointed out.

'I can't sleep.'

'Two insomniacs.'

'Insomniacs?'

'People who can't sleep.'

'Like zombies.' Maria couldn't tell Catherine how true it was. That at night she was like a zombie, that she was seeing things that frightened her.

'Do you want some whisky?' Catherine sat down next to her. 'Do you miss him?'

'Who?'

'The man you were in love with.'

'It's a long time. I forget.'

'I came to look for some paper. I'm going to write to Lilly to tell her I'm still alive and tell Hesketh that I'm sorry but I'm not coming back.'

'Hesketh was your boyfriend?'

'Yes. Fiancé, for a while.' She shivered, someone dancing on her grave. 'I used to call him the pencil man. He used to line his pencils up – all facing the same direction. He boiled his eggs for precisely four minutes in the morning and he put a blanket over his legs in the evening. It was ridiculous really. I don't know why I stayed so long.'

'What's he doing now?'

But Catherine didn't answer.

'Mr Fyncham has paper in his desk.' Maria closed her book.

Catherine went through to the study and turned on the light. She would tell Tom in the morning about the paper. She looked through his desk and found his leather writing case. There were only one or two pages of writing paper left and she hesitated before she tore them off the pad.

She didn't put the case back immediately, as she should have done, but started to look through the various compartments. Miss Berry from England, who had taught them at Hebron, had told her a cautionary tale about Fiddle fingers – Fiddle fingers had had her fingers chopped off.

She realised that what she was looking for was something personal of Tom's, that would help to explain him. A photograph of his wife or his family or the place that he came from. 'There must be something,' she thought. But there was nothing. Or nothing until she put the writing case back and saw the white edge of photographic paper sticking out of one of his farming books. She slid it out and held it up, but it wasn't of his wife, or his family or anyone.

She stared at it and a stone fell to the bottom of her stomach. It was so long ago – but she knew what it was, she was sure.

coffee and cakes and he had been called in to help because she couldn't cope. His father had gone into town.

Coffee meant one thing. Gossip. And this time there was something to gossip about. He saw their heads leaning in towards each other over the coffee table, like people watching an accident. They were whispering. 'She's come back.'

'Who?'

'Mr King's daughter.'

'I saw her driving up to the house. I didn't know who it was then. Of course I do now. I thought she was lost and I asked her – are you lost, I said. No, she said. I'm going to Hebron. I introduced myself. I thought it was the polite thing to do. Then she told me her name. Catherine King. I said not Mr King's daughter … and she said yes. And then you know what she said?'

They leant in again. 'What? What did she say?'

'She said, "I've come home." '

Nettie de Vries sunk back in her chair, triumphant.

'She didn't know then – about Mr and Mrs Fyncham?'

'Mrs Fyncham's left. I haven't seen her for two months now. The last time I saw her was in the chemist in town. She was buying medicines. You know I thought …'

'I've seen Mr Fyncham in town once or twice. Handsome man – like you see in the films.'

'Too handsome.'

'I don't trust handsome men.'

'Anyway, on that day when I first met Miss King, when I came back down the road later, her car was still there but there was no sign of her.'

'Where did she go?'

'I think she was up at that native church. I hate to think what goes on up there. They say it's *getoor*.'

'She's at the house now. Been living there. Moved in, like she'd never left. And he's still married. I don't want to think about what's going on in that house. It's not right with him married.'

'She just came back out of nowhere.'

'What happened to the wife? He doesn't look so upset, you know. It was very sudden. The way she disappeared.'

'I wouldn't want to be there when she gets back.' Nettie snorted.

'If she gets back.'

'What do you mean?'

'Well …'

There was a hush, but not for long.

'There's just the native girl at the house. You'd think she was white if you heard her on the phone. It's unnatural – like one of those ventriloquists at the circus.'

Nettie reached for another scone.

Hendrik wanted to make them stop. They knew nothing about Catherine and here they were picking like vultures over a carcass, ripping the skin off. His chest felt tight.

'And Ina saw them down by the river … laughing.'

'Where has she been all this time – the King girl?'

'The mother took them away. Father was caught – adultery, with another woman. He left the farm, never came back.'

Hendrik watched their faces. They seemed blurred. He could feel their words making the air a dirty brown, fogging it up so that it became thick. He went to open the window and stood with his back to them so that he could see out across the grass and the rolling hills and up to the ridge. He tried to fill his lungs and shut out their voices.

'I was driving past the store yesterday. She was at the farm school at Hebron with the picannins. She was barefoot. She's trying to teach them something. It's no use. Someone should tell her. It will only cause trouble and then she'll be sorry. You can't get too close; they'll be in the house, next thing they've taken everything.'

'What's that, Hendrik?' His mother looked up.

'I've got to go out,' he said.

His mother took his arm as he passed.

'But you haven't had your coffee. What's the matter?' Her eyes followed him as he left the room. He could hear Nettie de Vries.

'He's got so handsome. You must be proud of him.'

He went into the pantry and got two bottles of beer and put them in his bag. Then he ran out into the yard and kept running, down the path towards the koppies. His feet drummed on the ground. He listened to his breathing – in and out. He felt the heat on his head and the sweat sticking to his body.

He hummed to get their voices out of his head. The earth was warm under his feet. When he reached the koppie he lay under a tree, opened the beer and poured it down his throat. Their voices began to fade. Catherine would have finished at the school. She finished at lunchtime. She would be at the house or at the river. He would go up to the church and look down from the shelter of the trees into the pool and if she looked up he would wave at her and they would meet. He lit a cigarette and lay there thinking of Catherine. If he could just step through this clinging suffocating air into her world he felt sure he would be able to breathe freely.

He wasn't sure when he became conscious of their voices. He didn't sit up until they were quite close by, behind the rocks. Then he moved back under the tree into the shadows. They had stopped behind a big boulder and he moved forward so that he could hear them. It was the closest he had been to her.

Catherine laughed. Mr Fyncham must have said something funny.

Hendrik crept around the rock slowly, until he could see them, but they couldn't see him. They were sitting with their backs against the rocks, a little apart from each other. Her hair was wet. She picked a piece of grass and started chewing on it. Her skin was golden now from the sun; not pale like the day he had first seen her standing outside the church. And when he saw that she looked happy, his heart ached.

Mr Fyncham was peeling a mango with his knife. He handed her a piece – held it up to her mouth – but she took it with her fingers. She didn't want him touching her, Hendrik thought.

'Tell me what things you like.' Mr Fyncham asked her.

'What do you mean?' She was embarrassed, Hendrik could see. But she turned to Mr Fyncham and smiled and Hendrik saw the girl in the picture in the church.

'What things you like. It can't be that hard.' Mr Fyncham repeated. He was looking at her. She looked across the veld.

'Come on.'

'Why should I tell you? You never answer any of my questions, directly. Why so secretive Mr Fyncham?' But she was laughing.

'Okay, I'll tell you what I like. I like being here. With you.'

Hendrik watched as Mr Fyncham held out another piece of mango and she took it.

'And?'

'That's enough for me. And I like mangoes.'

Hendrik saw her face light up.

He would have asked her more questions. Small ones, big ones. He wanted to know all about her, he knew some of the answers already.

What's your favourite colour?

And what do you fear?

And what do you love?

He had seen her in the veld whirling round and round until she was dizzy. He had seen her running through the grass and swimming and lying stretched out on a rock staring up at the church.

'I like flying too ...' Mr Fyncham was looking up at Catherine now. She was standing over him, holding out her hand to pull him up.

'Why do you like flying so much?' She pulled him to his feet.

'Because I can forget everything when I'm up there.' He kept holding her hand.

'And what do you want to forget?' She couldn't look at him.

'Don't you ever give up? What is it you want from me?'

'Your body. Couldn't you guess?' And with that she turned and ran up the path ahead of him. Mr Fyncham ran after her.

'I'll race you to the top,' he shouted as he scrambled up the rocks. He was close behind her. Hendrik watched them until they disappeared from sight.

When he got back his mother was waiting for him.

'Where have you been? I was so worried.'

'I went for a walk.'

'I have a migraine.' She lowered herself into one of the chairs.

'I'll get you a drink of water.'

In the kitchen a fly had got caught and was buzzing against the fly mesh. Hendrik opened the window and let it out.

'Hendrik?'

'Coming Ma.'

He handed her the glass and sat down next to her. She sipped at the water.

'That's better.' She smiled at him. He felt sad.

Hendrik had a photograph of his mother when she was twenty-four. It was stuck to the inside of his cupboard. She was young and smiling and pretty, in a summer dress. Something had happened to her; he didn't know what. He remembered her chasing him through the long winter grass, making bird calls, making him laugh.

'You're a good boy, Hendrik. I should say young man. Seventeen is so grown up.' She patted his knee. 'I don't know what I'd do without you. You won't go too far away next year, will you? You know you could stay on the farm, your Pa could use the help.' She smiled at him. 'But then you must decide. You must do what you want. I only want you to be happy, you know?' Her voice trailed off.

'I'm going to be, Ma, soon.' He got up. 'I'm tired now, I'm going to lie down.'

'I'm also tired. I've been very tired all day now.' She sighed.

Hendrik lay in bed and stared at the ceiling. He must have slept for hours. When he woke up it was dark, his father was snoring and his mother was moving around the house.

★

Catherine was painting.

She had stumbled on the rocks on the path up to the church and Tom had put his hands around her waist to steady her and held them there. She had felt his chest against her back. And then he'd let her go. He was in her head now. He'd got in there and now he wouldn't leave. She hadn't wanted this to happen. He had a wife, he had the farm, and she didn't really know anything about him, but she wanted him to touch her again.

She squirted some black paint onto the palette. The sky should be darker and the moon brighter against the blue. She couldn't get it right.

There was a movement, a creak on the floorboards. Catherine looked up. Maria was standing in the doorway.

'What is it?' Catherine could see from her expression that something was wrong.

'I made lunch but you didn't come home. We were going to go to my mother's after lunch.'

'Oh God.' Catherine put her brush down and walked over to Maria. 'I finished teaching and I went down to the pool to swim, I was hot. And then Tom came down. We were there. I'm sorry. You should have come down.'

'I did.'

'Why didn't you call me? I was near the pool.'

'I didn't want to interrupt.'

'That's ridiculous. You know you're being ridiculous.' They had spent whole afternoons together. What was she supposed to do, ignore Tom entirely?

'Why don't you come and eat with us tonight?' she asked her.

Maria was polishing the edge of the bookshelf with her skirt. Catherine took her silence as a yes.

When Tom came back that night, Catherine could see he was annoyed that Maria was eating with them. He didn't say a word, nor did Maria and when Maria left the table he said, 'You see. She's uncomfortable eating with us.'

'She's not. She's making me feel guilty. I'll do something to make it right.'

'Just like that?' His tone was cutting. 'Is it that easy?'

'What's got into you?' She stood up.

'Nothing. I'm just tired. I'm going to read.' He wouldn't look at her.

It was then that the phone started ringing. They both listened. It was the ring for Hebron: two shorts, one long; two shorts, one long. Catherine got up to answer it, but Tom stopped her, grabbing her wrist. She had never answered the phone before at Hebron. Tom had said it was better not to and she had never questioned it, because she knew he was probably right. But she had written to Lilly and it might be her. And so what if it *was* Isobel? She had to know sometime.

'Leave it.' His grip made a red mark on her skin.

'Why? It might be for me. It might be Lilly.'

'I'll get it.'

She let him go.

Whoever was on the other end must have hung up. She could hear him. 'Hello, hello, who is this?'

'Who was it?' she asked him when he came back.

'They rung off.'

'They didn't say hello, there was nothing?'

'I said they rung off.'

He was out of the house. She went out after him but he had disappeared into the dark.

Maria was standing behind her.

'What is it?' she asked.

'He's gone off.'

'Was it Isobel?'

'I don't know. Probably. Sometimes the phone rings late at

night. He speaks to someone. He doesn't like me to answer the phone. He doesn't want her to know I'm here. He hasn't said that, but I know that.'

Maria couldn't tell Catherine about the dark room that she had seen at night in her sleep, or about Tom staring out into the sunlight and Isobel's hand on his arm, pulling him back.

'What are you going to do?'

'What can I do? Have a whisky or two or four. Will you join me?' Catherine poured herself and Maria one.

Maria would take Catherine's mind off Tom. She had done it before.

'Let's listen to some music. I have a record.' Maria went off to fetch Edmundo Ross and his big band.

It would be the two of them – they could dance. Catherine exclaimed when she saw the record sleeve with Edmundo Ross's face beaming up at them. 'I know this record. I used to dance to this, during the war. Here, I'll show you how the steps go. The rumba, the samba.' Catherine took Maria around the waist. 'I'll be the man. Just follow me.'

Maria laughed as they stumbled over each other's feet.

Round and round. Maria's head felt dizzy. When they got to the end of the song, they collapsed onto the floor.

'Tom used to dance.' Maria filled their glasses again. She shouldn't have said that. She must be drunk.

Catherine sat up. She was frowning. 'With Isobel?'

They had been having such fun.

'Just once. *She* wanted to.' Maria added quickly. She didn't want to spoil it now.

'What else did he do? Did he take her flying?'

'No.'

'Where does he go, when he goes out at night?'

'I don't know.'

The record had come to an end and the needle was scratching. Maria lifted it off and put Edmundo Ross back in his cover. They sat together and the silence settled around them.

'Do you remember in the beginning, the first wish we made in the church?'

Catherine looked at her.

'Yes.'

Catherine blew smoke rings, watching them lift in the air.

'Do you remember how it started?'

It had been at night. Catherine had held Maria's hand in the dark as they ran away from the house up to the church.

'Come on Katie.'

'Wait, I'm trying to find the torch.'

'What if someone see us?'

'They won't.'

'What if they hear us?'

'They won't. Not if you don't giggle.'

'I won't giggle. I think of my dead aunt.'

'You see. There you go, giggling. Stop it. I'll stuff a piece of cloth in your mouth.'

'You'll kill me. Then you'll be in trouble.'

'Okay. Let's synchronise watches.'

'I don't have a watch.'

'If we run and walk we'll get there faster without getting out of breath. Scouts do that.'

'Okay.'

'What if someone's up there?'

'They won't be.'

The church looked beautiful at night. The door was open and they walked in and stood there in the moonlight looking at the altar.

'The lady, she's not sing tonight.'

'She needs to sleep.'

'Now what?' Maria asked.

'Now we cut our fingers and mix our blood. 'I brought a knife.'

'A knife?'

'Come on.'

'And make a wish?'

'Yes.'

It was a simple wish. No harm in that. A wish to be friends, always.

★

It was late. Catherine must have fallen asleep on the couch. When she woke up she found that Maria had gone to bed. She got up and went down to Tom's room and knocked lightly on the door but there was no answer. Then she left the house and walked into the dark like they'd done that night. But this time she was alone. The avenue of gum trees was like a cathedral over her head. The leaves rustled. She ran down the dirt road, along the path to the pool and for a moment she forgot what age she was. She could almost hear Maria's laughter behind her on the path.

Tom was sitting on a rock with his legs in the water. She saw the glow of his cigarette. Then she walked to the edge of the water and started to take off her clothes. It was a challenge; it made her heart stronger.

'Do you want to swim?' she asked. *You can't do that Catherine. It's not appropriate.* She saw him crush out his cigarette and stand up. Then she jumped in. She swam away from him towards the far side of the pool and she didn't turn when she heard him jump in behind her.

He came up next to her. He took her hand under the water and she turned around. Then he held her head in his hands and kissed her. The feel of his tongue in her mouth shocked her for a second. He looked at her. She thought he was crying but she wasn't sure; it could have been the water.

She touched his cheek. 'I've got something to show you.'

'What is it?'

'Let's get dressed – it's up on the ridge.'

He followed her up the path to the church and inside. They stood in front of the photograph of herself. She shone her torch on it.

Then she slid her fingers between his.

'You haven't changed.' He looked at her. 'Not that much.'

'Will you kiss me here?'

'Why here? Is this a special place?' He was amused.

She couldn't explain.

'I just want you to.'

They sat together on the floor. He held her in his arms. She shut her eyes.

'What's the matter?' he asked her.

'Nothing.'

'Are you sure?'

'Nothing.'

They didn't talk on the way back to the house but he held her hand. When they got back they sat on the stoep. He kissed her again. Then he told her that he had to go away, not for long, he said, just for a few days, just to sort something out.

'I can tell you everything when I get back.'

'Do you love her?' She had said it.

'It's not like that,' he said, 'it's complicated. I … you'll be here when I get back, won't you?'

'Yes.'

'I'll miss you. Next time you must come with me. Have you ever eaten prawns?'

'No.'

'There are so many things to show you. All the places I've been, I want to show you. Will you sleep with me tonight?' he asked her.

She hesitated.

'Just lie with me.'

She curled up next to him but her mind was racing. There had been something in the church – something different. She had felt alone – she had never felt alone there before, she shouldn't have felt that. She couldn't make it out. He put his arm around her and pulled her towards him in his sleep.

Seven

In her dream Catherine is searching for Tom in the old quarter of a city by the sea. The air is humid and the vegetation is tropical. The city is crumbling. Houses that used to be grand, stand derelict. Plants grow wild in courtyards. Pools and fountains are empty of water. Leaves have collected on the cracked concrete. She is walking down a narrow cobbled street that leads down to the water. Her feet are bare. There is no one out on the streets, but when she looks up at the buildings she sees washing hanging from balconies and she can smell cooking.

At the bottom of the street she comes across an old fortress. She has seen it somewhere before but she can't think where. It's familiar to her, like family. The walls are crumbling and palm trees grow in the centre square. The steps lead down into the turquoise sea. The tide is high. She knows this because the water covers the sand in front of the building and laps on the bottom steps. The water looks inviting. She could take off her dress and slide into it but she is searching for someone. For Tom.

She hears the sound of children laughing nearby, but she can't see them. Out on the ocean dhows are bobbing up and down. She looks down and sees that the roughness under her feet is because she is standing on a pile of fish scales. She turns down towards where the children are playing. There is a small square lined with pepper trees. A little black girl in a tattered dress is chasing a boy around; he has stolen the mango she was eating.

A group of women are standing around a stone slab, gutting fish. A man comes over with a bucket of fish and empties it onto the slab. The women laugh and shout at him in a language she doesn't understand. She walks up to them but they don't seem to see her.

She is in a house. It is cool inside off the street. There are tiles under her feet. In front of her a staircase leads up to the first floor. There is a long dark passage with rooms leading off it and at the end a closed door in front of her. She wants to stop, to go back down the passage and run out into the light and heat of the street, but is compelled to keep on walking towards the closed door and, when she gets to it, open it.

There is a bed and two bodies, lying naked in each other's arms.

Tom looks up at her over his wife's shoulder. They both stare at her as if she is an intruder.

★

Maria was beside Tom's bed, shaking Catherine's arm. 'You were shouting in your sleep.' Catherine sat up and covered her face with her hands.

'I had a bad dream.' She looked around the room. 'Where's Tom?' And then she remembered that he had gone away.

'What happened?' Maria sat down on the edge of the bed. 'I went to your room but you weren't there.'

'I went to the pool. I found him there. Now he's gone.'

'Why were you shouting?'

'In my dream, he was with her. I found them together.' Catherine got up and went to open the curtains and the windows. 'I don't want to think about it. I'm going to go down to the pool. I need to clear my head.'

Maria stared out of the window; she didn't look at Catherine when she spoke.

'Breakfast is ready. Gabriel wants to know what to do in the garden today. Mr Fyncham told him to come up here this morning.'

'Tell him I'll be out in ten minutes. Go on …'

★

Hendrik was lying in the grass watching the road into town. He could see the school bus coming closer. It stopped every morning where the road from Zevenfontein met the tar road and Dirk, Hendrik and Elise, the girl from Tweefontein, got on to go to school in town. Hendrik had been early. Dirk and Elise weren't at the meeting place when he got there, and instead of waiting at the side of the road he had ducked down into the ditch out of sight. He watched Dirk's father drop Dirk and Elise off.

People said Elise was simple, but Hendrik knew she was just different. He understood because he was different too. The boys teased her at school. They pulled her plaits and tried to goad her into speaking when she didn't want to.

Now she sat on her school satchel and drew in the earth with a stick. The bus stopped next to them. Elise got on and Dirk looked around, obviously wondering where Hendrik was, but the bus couldn't wait. Hendrik watched from his hiding place as it drove off. He lay on his back at the side of the road for a long time after the bus had gone, watching the kestrels circling on the thermals overhead, round and round, soaring higher and higher, then plummeting to the earth.

He knew how to fly, not up there in an aeroplane, but he had flown at night. Once he had woken up on the floor.

He watched the sun rising in the sky. He was completely peaceful. He didn't need to go to school, not for what he wanted to do. He knew how to farm, he knew how to draw, and he knew that he was going to meet Catherine King. When the sun got too hot he got up and started to walk back across the veld. He took his shirt off and wrapped it around his head like a turban. His body was brown from the sun.

The church was still cool inside when he got there, but it was going to heat up quickly and then he would have to go down into the trees above the pool to keep cool.

*

Catherine floated in the water.

A bishop bird flew down low across the pool. Its heavy tail fluttered as it hovered and then disappeared in the reeds. Catherine swam to the side and pulled herself up on the rocks. Her senses seemed sharper. She felt the colours. She could taste the sweetness on the air: the earth in the water and smell of the trees above her.

Hendrik watched Catherine from the trees – and then she looked up and saw him and he lost his footing and slid down the bank. He cut his leg against a rock as he fell and cried out. He tried to stand but his ankle had twisted and he winced. The skin had split open on his calf and he was bleeding badly.

Catherine was calling to him from the bank. She was drying herself with a towel. 'Are you all right? Don't move. I'll come up. Just wait there.'

He hadn't wanted to meet her like this. He had wanted them to meet in the church. 'It's okay,' he called and tried to drag himself up the bank, but she was already scrambling up the path to the church. He watched as she made her way between the trees. She had pulled on a dress but her feet were bare and there was grass in her hair. She squatted down beside him and looked at the cut.

'We can use your shirt to stop the bleeding. Tom had a cut like this and it wasn't as bad as …' She stopped. He had unwrapped his shirt from his head and she wrapped it around his leg and tied it securely.

'It's not bad,' he told her. But when he stood up he stumbled.

'Where are you from?' she asked him. And he told her how he had come walking from Zevenfontein, that he was on his way down to the river on the other side of the ridge – he hoped she didn't mind him passing across her land.

Maria had told Catherine about the boy who was strange, the boy who went to the church at night.

'You can't walk like that. Put your arm around my neck. I'll help you back to Hebron. It's not far. We can clean your cut, then I can drive you home.'

'I don't want to trouble you …'

'It's no trouble. I'm not busy. Tom … Here let me carry your bag.'

He had forgotten about his bag. He carried it with him always. It contained his sketchbook and pencils, matches and cigarettes and sometimes a bottle of paraffin wrapped in plastic bags for the lamp in the church.

Catherine took it and slung it over her shoulder. Then she put her arm around his waist to support him. His right arm rested over her shoulders. They were touching, he had just met her and they were touching, she had her arm around him and he could smell her skin and her hair and feel her warm body.

They made slow progress with him hopping beside her – stopping every few yards to rest. He was aware that he was sweating and that she would smell the sweat and it made him awkward. It was better when they had inched their way down the slope and reached the flat ground at the bottom. They rested there and she fetched him some water to drink. Then they set out down the path. It seemed to take forever to reach the house. She asked him about his farm, what they farmed, and if he often went to the church.

When they got to Hebron, Catherine called for Maria and went to look for her while Hendrik waited, but she came back alone.

'If you come through to the bathroom I'll wash the cut with some antiseptic.'

It was the first time Hendrik had been inside the house at Hebron. The house of sin – as his mother and her friends described it. The nearest he had been was the gate, where he had stood and watched in the dark. He had heard the music and seen the curtains blowing in the breeze when all the windows were flung open on hot nights. He had watched them walking in and out of the house and heard the murmur of conversation. One night he had had to duck down into the shadows as Tom Fyncham walked past him down the road. On another occasion the native girl had been picking spinach in the garden in the dark and had stood up and looked straight at him.

The windows were open and a door led off the big room onto the courtyard at the back. He could smell flowers. Someone had picked roses and put them in a vase on the piano. A radio was playing in the kitchen. The chairs had cloths thrown over them – they looked like they came from foreign places. There were leather cushions and a silver tray with a coffee pot. Against one wall someone had hung a long string of beads that the native women made on the farms.

When Catherine took Hendrik through to the courtyard he could see she had started painting a mural on one of the walls. The colours were vivid like the slash of a red bird in the dry grass.

A prickly pear tree grew in the centre of the courtyard, and euphorbia trees and roses in beds between the slates. He could smell the scent in the heat. It was still in the centre of the house, slow in the heat, just the buzzing of insects. The bathroom was cool. Catherine went to fetch a chair that he could sit on while she washed the cut. She filled a basin of water and he rested his foot in it. She didn't speak while she washed and cleaned his cut; she seemed absorbed in what she was doing. He was conscious of her hands on his skin. She dried his leg with a towel and wrapped a bandage around the wound.

'You should put the shirt in water to soak, to get the blood out, when you get home.' She stood up and looked at the job she'd done.

'I'll get you one of Tom's shirts.'

'Don't worry, really.'

'You can bring it back when you can.' Catherine wondered what Maria would think of the strange boy being in the house. She would have probably left him to bleed or to find his own way home. She opened Tom's cupboard and started sorting through the shirts to find one suitable for the boy, one Tom wouldn't mind her using. He didn't have many clothes but those he did have were neatly folded. She found a suit hanging at the back of the cupboard that she had never seen him wear. She remembered Maria telling her about his shoes when she had first seen him step out of the car. They were city shoes.

Hendrik took the shirt from Catherine. As he put it on he felt something small and hard in the pocket. He took it out and held it out to her. It was a hard white disk with a fine dotted pattern on it. She didn't take it from him. She just stared.

'What is it?' he asked.

'It's a pansy shell,' she said slowly. 'You find them at the coast on the beach.' Then she took it from him and turned it over in her hand. 'I used to have one when I was a girl; I found it when we went on holiday.' She held it out for him to look at again.

'It's beautiful,' he said.

'We called them sea dollars.'

'Underwater money,' he laughed.

'I'll put it here.'

She placed it on the window ledge above the bath.

'So it can be near water.' And then he wished he hadn't said that. He'd said so many stupid things.

'The shirt looks good on you, it's a bit big but …'

'I'll send it back as soon as I can. Won't Mr Fyncham mind? Please, I should ask him.'

'He's not here. He's gone away for a few days.' She was trying to wash the blood out of his shirt. Eventually she left it to soak.

'How does your leg feel?'

He took a few limping steps.

'I'll get my car and take you home.'

'It's okay.'

'You can't walk. Really, I'd like to.'

They drove in silence down the avenue and round the back roads to the gate to his farm. He could see his father's truck outside the house.

'I'll walk from here.' He turned to her. She could see that he didn't want to be embarrassed being brought home by the English woman who was living with a married man at Hebron. She had seen the looks they gave her in town. He would have to explain.

'It was nice to meet you …' she held out her hand to shake his, and realised that she didn't know his name.

'Hendrik. And you too, Miss King – Catherine,' he said tentatively. 'I'll bring the shirt back.' He hesitated. 'And thank you,' he said as he got out of the car.

She watched him limping back to the farmhouse. A woman came out onto the driveway to meet him. She looked towards the car, but she didn't wave.

When Catherine got back to the house the phone was ringing, but by the time she reached it, it had stopped. It was Tom, she felt sure, he said he would call.

She went to look for Maria and found her in the kitchen slicing up rhubarb.

'I hope you're not using pineapple with that.' Catherine observed. 'They say it's deadly.'

'Where did you find him?' Maria looked up at her. 'The Afrikaans boy.'

'I didn't find him. He was up near the church. He cut his leg and I brought him here to bandage it, then I drove him home.'

'He was watching you swimming in the river.'

'For all I know he was walking down to the ledge to go swimming himself. He seemed sensitive and gentle. And what's the matter with you? You sound like a private investigator?'

This got a laugh from Maria. She dried her hands on her skirt and then reached for a parcel on the table. She passed Catherine Hendrik's bag. 'He left this behind,' she said.

'Could you drop it off when you go to your mother's place?' Catherine didn't take it.

'Have you seen what's inside?' Maria wanted her to look. She wanted Catherine to know how strange the boy was.

'I'm not going to look.'

'There's a drawing book in there. You should see the drawings.'

'What about them?'

'Look at them.'

'No. I'm going to put it in the study. I think you need to get out of the house. You're getting paranoid. Let's go to a film in town after lunch?'

'I can't go to the cinema with you. You always forget. I'm black.'

'Well, then, we'll buy a bottle of wine and we'll go for a drive to the waterfall. And you can drive.'

*

It was just the two of them in the car. Maria drove along the dirt roads with the windows wide open and the wind rushing in and the dust flying up: first gear, second gear, third gear, fourth gear, heaven.

Catherine opened the bottle of wine with a penknife and put on the radio. 'Slow down, Maria, you'll kill us.'

Maria had learnt to drive remarkably fast, as though she had remembered something that had been forgotten.

Up and up, onto the escarpment and the land fell away on either side down into valleys. The clouds got closer and closer.

In that bubble of sound and dust and light Maria could have stayed forever with Catherine. She could take a photograph of them together in the car on the road and live in it always. Just her and Catherine going places together. She wished it could always be like that.

When they got back to the house that evening Catherine jumped up every time the phone rang, but it was never the ring for Hebron. Maria watched her waiting for the call that didn't come from Tom.

Eventually Catherine got up from where she had been trying to read and said she was going to bed. She had read the same sentence ten times without taking anything in.

Later, on her way back from the church, Maria saw the light on in the study and she knew Catherine was in there looking through the Afrikaans boy's sketches – looking for something that would tell her more about Tom. Perhaps the boy had seen something, she would be thinking.

Catherine turned the pages of Hendrik's sketchbook, slowly tracing her fingers across the scenes. She recognised everything that he had drawn because it was on the farm: the cabbage trees, the rocks in the koppies where she and Maria had played, the river, the birds in the reeds. They were beautiful sketches, far better than anything she had ever done. Then, when she turned to the back of the book, she found more. These were sketches he had done separate from the rest.

He had drawn the church. It was an interior view of the altar and, in the back, the baptismal font and next to it a girl, standing, smiling at him, that skew smile with the gap between her teeth. She was holding a cosmos flower. He had even drawn the peacocks embroidered on the hem of her dress and her bare feet.

Catherine turned the page. There was the river pool, and in it a woman swimming naked. Her hair spread out around her in the water. He had drawn Isobel Fyncham. He had known her. Catherine closed the book and sat for a while trying to make sense of it. Then she went to Tom's desk to fetch writing paper.

Dear Hendrik,

You forgot your bag.

She tore the paper up and started again.

If you would like me to help you with your sketching meet me at the river pool on Saturday.

She folded the letter up and slipped it inside the sketchbook and then put the book back in his bag. She would ask Maria if she would take it when she went that way.

Eight

Hendrik's mother found her son's bag when she got back from the shops. Maria had left it on the table. Hendrik was out helping his father on the land. She took the sketchbook out, opened it and found the letter.

When Hendrik came home his mother could see excitement on his face. She had put the sketchbook back in the bag. He sat down and put his leg up on a stool. 'Is it better?' she asked, noticing how the wound had closed, there would be a scar.

'This was here when I got in.' She handed him the bag. He took it to his room. She waited for him to come back out and tell her about the sketches and what they meant. She wanted to know what he had being doing with that woman at Hebron, but when he did come out, he just went through to the kitchen and made himself some coffee and sat down to read a book.

'Hendrik,' she paused, 'I didn't know you sketched.'

He looked up quickly. His face was angry.

'It was on the table,' she said, almost pleadingly, 'I thought you wouldn't mind.'

'It was private, Ma.' He got up and went to his room. She followed him down the passage but he closed the door on her. Half an hour later he went out.

*

Hendrik had the letter in his pocket, and his sketchbook. He rode and shouted into the wind. The further he rode away from the farm the lighter he felt until he began to laugh.

Miss King wanted to see him, she was going to teach him to draw and paint, he was going to meet her by the river pool. She wanted him. She had seen his sketches and she thought they were good and Mr Fyncham had gone away. Nothing else mattered.

The church was quiet. He found a place on the floor and opened his sketchbook. Then he closed his eyes and held his pencil over the paper. He could feel their breath as they leaned closer over his shoulder and watched as he let the pencil move across the page.

★

'Katie.' Catherine opened her eyes. Maria was standing next to her bed.

'You called for me in your sleep.'

'How long have I been asleep?' Catherine sat up in bed, her head heavy and confused. 'Has Tom come back? I thought I heard a car.'

'That was the man who delivers paraffin.'

Catherine got up. 'What if she comes back?' she asked Maria.

'She's not going to.'

'What if she does? If she comes back when he's away? Or with him?'

'She won't.'

'How do you know? Have you seen something? Have you?'

Maria shook her head. 'I've made tea and there's cake. Your favourite cake.'

Maria cut the cake into slices. She didn't tell Catherine that she had seen Mrs Scholtz opening Hendrik's sketchbook and watched the expression on her face when she read the letter. She didn't tell Catherine about the phonecall either. The one that came that morning, from far away. The crackling line. She had put it down in fright, before the person could say hello.

Catherine finished her tea and set off for the school. Maria watched her go.

When Catherine was with the children and they were asking her questions and pulling her skirt and laughing, she could forget that Tom wasn't there.

When she came back up to the house she asked Maria for scissors. Maria looked alarmed.

'What are you going to do?'

'Cut off my hair. You know, people do that in traumas.' They laughed.

When Maria came out into the garden an hour later to see what Catherine had done, she found her standing in the middle of the bed of dahlias. She had cut off all the heads.

'I've always hated dahlias, all those frills, puffed up and fussy. It looks much better like this, doesn't it?'

'You're crazy.' But Maria was smiling. Mrs Fyncham had liked them so much – those dahlias. She had made Gabriel plant a whole bed of them.

'I feel better though.' Catherine looked around her. She looked better too, Maria thought, less anxious.

'What are you going to do with them?' Maria walked through the scattered heads, her feet black against the bright yellow and pink.

'I thought we'd drown them in the bath, just to make sure.'

They sat down on the wall and looked at the flowers.

'I'll take them home. My sister will love them,' Maria said.

'We'll go together, tonight.'

'We can go now.' Maria had started collecting the flowers in her skirt.

'I can't go now. I said I'd meet the Afrikaans boy by the pool. I said I'd help him with his sketching.'

Maria watched as Catherine packed a bottle of wine. She couldn't stop her, Catherine was determined. 'I'm taking wine; it's a picnic. I'm also taking cheese and bread. There's nothing wrong with that,' she said defiantly.

'Why not strawberries? That's what they always eat in the books on picnics. They feed each other strawberries.' Maria's tone was sarcastic.

'We haven't got any strawberries.' Catherine knew she shouldn't be doing this, but she couldn't stop, she had to know what he had seen.

Maria watched as Catherine walked down to the stables. She didn't offer to help carry the basket or the bag with Catherine's sketching things. Catherine turned around at the gate. 'You'll call me if he comes back, won't you? You'll come down to the pool and fetch me?' Maria didn't answer.

Catherine wanted to get to the pool before Hendrik. It was her river, he was the visitor. She had to be in control of this. When she got to the pool she spread out the blanket and put the food out and the wine in the water to cool. Then she got out her sketching block and pencils so that she would seem busy when he arrived. It would seem professional. She was an artist; she was going to help him to sketch. The sun was baking down and she was thirsty so she opened the bottle of wine and poured herself a glass. It was a bad time to meet, there would be only a small patch of shade which meant he would have to squash up next to her on the blanket. She had brought Tom's clock so that she would know how long they had been sketching. It would be professional.

⋆

Hendrik went over the events of the afternoon again. He had changed his shirt four times. He had packed his bag and unpacked it. His mother had stopped him when he reached the driveway. She had been sitting out on the stoep, quite still, staring blankly in front of her. He didn't know how long she had been there.

'I'm worried, Hendrik.'

'You mustn't worry, Ma.'

'How can I not worry? You mustn't go there Hendrik – to that church, to Hebron. I have a bad feeling about it. Things are going on over there that …'

'Ma.'

'Promise me.' She looked at his bag. 'Where are you going with that?'

'I'm going to meet Dirk down at the river.'

'Can I come too?' She stood up. 'It's been so long since I went to the river. Remember how your father and us used to go down there. But you don't want your mother along with you now.'

'It's not that, Ma.' He was going to be late, he might miss Catherine. He had to get away from the house.

⋆

But when he got to the wattle trees and looked down at the pool she was there, lying on a blanket in her bathing costume. From the trees above the pool it looked as if she was sleeping. He couldn't see her face, just the back of her head and her hair spread out on the blanket and he hurried down the path, approaching her slowly, trying not to make a noise. He wondered whether to call her, but he just said her name under his breath, trying it out: 'Catherine, Miss King.' There was no reason he should startle her if he moved quietly closer until he was right by her.

'Catherine?'

He *had* frightened her.

'It's okay.' He put his hand out as he would to an animal that was trapped.

'Oh, it's you.' She sat up. 'I must have fallen asleep. I thought it was someone else.' She looked dazed. He sat quietly waiting for her to be ready to talk to him. He poured her a cup of water. She leant back against the tree and he sat down on the edge of the blanket.

'It's hot,' he said. It sounded so stupid. But she didn't seem to have heard. She got up and walked to the rocks at the edge of the pool.

'This will wake me up!' She turned and beckoned to him. 'Why don't you come in?'

'I'll watch you.' Another silly thing to say. She would think that he had been spying on her. She jumped into the water.

'Come in,' she called to him. He had a towel in his bag. He tried to crouch behind the tree to take off his shorts with the towel tied around his waist. It was ridiculous. She was on the far side of the pool. She must be sitting on a submerged rock, because he could see her legs. He ran and dived in and grazed his arms against a rock. When he broke the surface she was swimming towards him. 'You have to be careful. There are only certain places in the pool where you can dive. There are rocks underwater. Are you all right?' She was treading water next to him, in the deepest part of the pool.

'It's just a graze.'

'You must be accident prone.' He didn't understand. 'You have a lot of accidents.'

'Only around you,' he thought, but he just nodded. He swam a bit so that she could get out and dry herself and change. Then he got out and wrapped a towel around himself.

'Here.' She handed him a glass of wine.

They talked about the weather, about farming. Then she asked him if he'd brought his sketchbook. He took it out. 'Let me see the sketches again.'

He handed her the book. She could see that he was nervous. She felt nervous too, but for a different reason. It was because she shouldn't be doing this, because she liked him; and he was so young and gullible. 'Would you like one?' She offered him a cigarette. He took one and she lit it for him and their fingers touched. He coughed when he inhaled. 'They're very strong, I know,' she laughed.

He loved the sound of her voice.

'You've been up to the church often?' She was paging through his sketches.

He didn't know whether it was a statement or a question. 'Yes.' They both looked at the sketch he'd done of the church of the little girl standing in the doorway. She didn't ask who it was, perhaps she knew.

'I saw you there,' he said. 'You've got the same smile.'

She looked at him. 'I was eight when that picture was taken.'

'Did you play there in the church; because …' He hesitated.

'Because?' There was an edge to her voice.

'Nothing. I just wondered.'

Then she relaxed. He could feel it, an easing in the air. 'When I was a girl I used to hide in the church. Sometimes Maria and I would go up there at night. We used to play up in those trees. One day we scrambled down to the ledge and dared each other to jump off into the pool.'

'And did you?'

'Yes. We learnt to swim in this pool.'

'I also learnt in this river, but further down, where it runs through our farm. By the bridge.'

'I know that place.'

'Have you got brothers and sisters?'

'No.'

'You're all alone then.' He felt she was looking right through him. 'I am too.'

'I thought you had a sister?' He looked up and saw that she was frowning.

'We're not close,' she said.

'Your father?'

'He's dead.'

'I'm sorry. He must have been very sad to leave this place.'

'Yes.' She turned the page in the sketchbook. There was the woman swimming in the river pool. Naked. 'This is here?'

'Yes.' He had trespassed on her land.

'It's a beautiful composition.' She paused. 'Who is it?' She was looking at him now, straight into his eyes and past into his heart. He looked away.

'It's Mrs Fyncham.' He couldn't tell Catherine the truth – that it was her, Catherine. That he watched her from the trees above the pool when she swam. That it made his heart ache. That Mr Fyncham had been in the pool with her, but he had shaded him out.

'Did you know Mrs Fyncham? I should say, do you know her?' She tried to make it sound light.

'She used to come swimming here – I met her here once or twice.' He was getting out of his depth now.

'And she was naked?' She was teasing him now.

'She liked to swim like that.'

'And she didn't mind you drawing her naked?' She saw him shift and she wanted to stop, because she liked him, but she couldn't.

'Her husband – he asked me to paint her. He wanted a portrait of her.' Catherine didn't say anything. When he looked at her, she had gone pale. 'Are you all right?' It was such a mess now. He had made a mess of it.

'They came down here together?'

'Yes. They met here, after he'd finished work. They liked to swim.'

'She didn't tell you why she left?'

He'd said the wrong thing. It was not entirely a lie – he had seen Mrs Fyncham at the pool but not with Tom. It had been late one night, soon before she left. She had stood on the ledge above the pool looking down into the dark water.

There was a long silence. Hendrik struggled with what to say next. 'You belong here. It's where you are.' He hesitated. 'It's where I am too.'

Then he asked her to show him how to sketch, to cover his confusion. She suggested they start on the pool. She handed him a sheet. He pressed it against his sketchbook. It was good paper, not like his cheap book. He started to draw. 'Relax,' she told him. 'Stop frowning.'

She got her paper out and looked at the pool. She saw different colours in the water and the reeds moving at the edge. But now, when she looked at the water, she saw Isobel swimming in the pool. She watched as she dived and surfaced. Her black hair was sleek against her head. She was laughing, calling Tom. 'Come in, why don't you join me?'

Catherine looked at her paper and saw that she had drawn a figure in the water. She wiped it out, smudging it with the back of her hand. She started to draw again. The cliff rising out of the water, the bushes clumped at the top, the darkness of the rocks, the arms of the trees. She would replace her. She would draw them at the pool, Maria and her, two figures playing in the shallows. Two little girls naked, bent over looking at pebbles under the water. Intent, absorbed, uncaring, happy.

They started to talk as they sketched. She told him about the places she'd gone as a child. The time passed quickly. She looked at his picture and suggested where he could lighten it and where he could shade more. It was so much better than hers was; he should have been the one helping her. Then it was time to pack up. 'Would you like to do this again? Do you think it helped?' she asked.

'Oh yes.' His heart was singing.

'Shall we meet next Saturday then, here?' They separated where the path forked. He watched her walk away from him through the grass.

Nine

Maria noticed the change in Catherine when she came back from the river. The Afrikaans boy had told her something that she hadn't wanted to hear. Maria had warned her not to go. Catherine told Maria that she would meet her at her mother's place later, she just wanted to sit for a while. She watched Maria as she walked off down the driveway. Maria turned back and waved from the gate. She didn't want to leave Catherine there but she knew that she wanted to be alone. Tom still hadn't called.

Catherine watched the colours changing as the light faded. She heard the sounds of the workers shouting in the distance and watched the children running down the dirt road past the house. A peacock was calling from the trees.

As it got dark, the fires stood out – orange pinpoints in the veld, beacons in a sea of darkness.

Tom was out there in the dark, getting closer, moving further away, bringing her in, shutting her out.

Maria was out there waiting for her, singing a made-up song, memorising strange facts from books to make her laugh, sitting on her lover's grave, sitting alone by the water staring up at the aeroplane in the sky, watching the ants crawling on the red earth.

Hendrik was in the church, his pencil dancing across the pages, his heart singing.

Isobel was out there, swallowed up by some dark hole, trying to find her way back.

And the girls were up in the church, tracing circles in the dust, laughing their fears away, turning the dark into a pirate's ship, a wedding, a baptism, a flower in a vase, a wish.

The Swazi words were coming back to her now, slowly forming themselves into sentences. Some were too far away to hold on to. They were words she would need to talk to Maria's mother. Tom had been gone for ten days and he hadn't called. She was angry that she wanted him to call so badly, and angry that he hadn't. She wanted him to come back. Maria was there, but she still felt lonely. It wasn't enough. It had been, but it wasn't now. She got a jersey and pulled it on over her dress and took a torch from the cupboard, then set out for Maria's mother's kraal. What she remembered of Maria's mother was warmth.

She smells of menthol, she uses it for her chest. Her apron is faded, her knees stained with floor polish. I lean back against her big warm body.

'My naughty girls,' she laughs. 'Where were you? Madam was looking for you. Calling everywhere.' Her arms fold around me. I could fall asleep. I don't need sheep. I feel her chest, rising and falling, rising and falling. She straps Lilly on her back when she cleans in the house. 'Where were you? She sent Philemon to look for you down at the store.'

'We were hunting.'

'If the house burns down. If there's a big veld fire, like last winter.'

'A runaway fire. A fire that is running away, from what?'

'Be serious, Maria. If everyone is burnt, we'll have to find our own food.'

'We'll be hunter-gatherers. I'll be the gatherer. I know what you can eat in the veld.'

'No you don't, Maria. You nearly killed us with that plant you made us eat. No, I'll hunt things with my stick.'

'What will you hunt?'

'Sheep.'

'You don't have to hunt sheep. They are a domestic animal. If you catch one you have to kill it.'

'Why me?'

'Because you the hunter. Can you kill something?'

'I don't know.'

'My mother kill chickens. She chop their heads off and they run around. She kill a goat, cut its neck with a knife. An old knife.'

'Don't tell me that. I don't want to hear about it.'

'You could try kill something small. Like a mouse, when the cat brings it in and it's still alive but it's dying. You can practise on that. Or a frog.'

'Yugh.'

'You can hit with a rock. You can't wait. He who hesitates is lost.'

'What?'

'I read it in a book at the house.'

'You're crazy.'

They laugh.

⋆

Two mangy dogs came tearing out of the dark barking as Catherine approached Maria's mother's hut. They stood snarling at her until a man came out with a stick and chased them away. He took off his battered hat and nodded at her and she greeted him. Maria had come to the entrance of the hut.

The inside of the hut was smoky. There was a paraffin lamp burning and she could make out the shape of a child sitting on a steel bed in the corner. Other children crowded around her, touching her skirt, wanting to feel her hair. She knew two of them from the school. Maria's mother sat in the corner on a mat. She had shrunken with age. When Catherine got closer she could see that one eye was milky from cataracts. She held up her hand and Catherine took it and squatted down next to her.

'*Maye ba bo*, Katie, you grow so beautiful. Let me look.' She clicked her tongue. Then she told Maria to bring a chair, two chairs; they couldn't entertain a guest like this. Maria helped her mother up and she sunk down on the chair, the broken riempies sagging under her. Catherine recognised the chairs as old ones from Hebron. There were also a couple of old china pots that her mother had given Maria's mother because they were broken. They had been given pride of place in an old cabinet.

'Let me look at you,' she said again and studied Catherine's face. 'Maria can make tea.' She turned to Maria and spoke to her in Swazi. 'Bring the proper cups out,' she told her. 'Katie, it's been such a long time. How's mummy?'

'She's dead, Mama. I told you.' Maria was rummaging in a drawer. She brought out a box – full of old tissue paper. Inside were china cups; they were old ones with chips from the house at Hebron. 'I tell her all the time, but she forgets.' Maria poured water into the cups and took an old tin with a picture of the King and Queen on it. There was one tea bag left and she squeezed it against the side of the cup and used it again in the next one. The tea was a milky colour – Maria had this one.

'I'm sorry, Katie.' The old woman squeezed Catherine's hand. 'Your mother was a kind somebody. She taught me English. But I'm forgetting everything.' She laughed, waving her hands, and started coughing again. 'It's hard now. I can't work. There's no money. The two eldest are on the mines. And Maria's so rude to men.' Maria rolled her eyes. 'Are you married? Baas Fyncham is handsome. I saw you down by the river with him yesterday. I went to look for mushrooms down there in the veld. He's a good man.'

'Mama, you didn't go out yesterday.'

'It was yesterday. You weren't here. I'm not stupid. I went down to the pool. I saw Katie with him.' She reached out and touched Catherine's hair. 'But you changed your hair. I think it was long; it was different and the colour was dark.'

'You're getting confused, Mama. She can't remember when things happened. That wasn't yesterday, Mama.' Maria got up to fetch water from the bucket in the corner for her mother, who was coughing again. 'She saw Mr and Mrs Fyncham once down by the river.' Maria explained to Catherine.

'I know what I saw.' Her mother was getting agitated now. 'Why don't you use a proper teapot. Not this old thing.' She made

Maria look for another teapot. She was getting tired. Catherine could see. After tea Catherine said goodbye and promised to come again. Maria's mother hobbled out into the yard. 'My two naughty girls,' she called after them. 'All grown up.' She waved them off into the dark.

⋆

They walked in silence for a while. Catherine led the way with the torch and Maria followed her. Catherine could hear Maria humming under her breath. That silly clapping song.

Down by the bramble bushes
Down by the sea
Boom boom boom …

'When I die I want you to check that I'm really dead before they put me in the coffin.'

Catherine turned around to look at Maria.

'I'm serious,' Maria said.

'But they'll know you're dead. You'll stop breathing.'

'But to make sure. Sometimes they make mistakes. There are stories I've read about claw marks on coffins. You have to check for a pulse but you've got to wait a while because it might have slowed down. I read about a turtle that was caught in a net, its heart beat once every hour.'

'That's a turtle. You read too much, Maria.'

'You can hold a glass up to my mouth to see if I'm breathing.'

'Why are we talking about this anyway?'

'Because I want to know that you'll do that when I die.'

'You're my age. You're not going to die.'

'You never know. Think of my aunt, run over when she was crossing the road. There's murder as well.'

'Why would anyone want to kill you?'

'But say they did, for some reason.'

'This is a stupid conversation to be having.'

'But will you? If you say yes, I'll stop.'

'Yes, I'll check to make sure you're dead. But what if I die first?'

'Will you leave me your car?'

Catherine laughed. They had reached the school when she stopped in her tracks and Maria nearly bumped into her. 'Who else will drive it?' Maria went on, but Catherine wasn't listening, she was staring up the driveway to the house. It was lit up in the dark and there was music playing. She began to run, leaving Maria standing in the road.

The door was open and Catherine ran up the flight of steps and went inside. She stopped when she saw what was on the armchair in the middle of the room and stared. Suddenly she couldn't hear the record playing or Maria calling or the dogs barking or Tom's voice. She could only see down a tunnel and at the end where a green jacket and a black handbag were so casually thrown down on a chair, as if the owner had returned from a day's shopping and gone to run the bath.

Ten

Tom was standing in the doorway. He had walked in from the courtyard with just a towel wrapped around his waist – he must have been in the bath. 'Catherine?' he sounded surprised. He came towards her. She was still staring at the chair. His tone was so offhand as if nothing had happened between them. She thought of the night at the river pool and the thing he hadn't been able to tell her. She would have to leave now. She had made a horrible mistake. 'Oh, you found them.' He gestured to the jacket and bag. 'I didn't mean you too. It was to be a surprise.'

'A surprise?' She felt sick in her stomach. He had brought Isobel back. It had meant nothing, all the rest.

'Obviously a bad one. You should have warned me you don't like surprises.'

She didn't hear him.

'Where is she?'

'Where is who?'

'Your wife.' She couldn't say her name.

'It's a present, Catherine. It's just a present. I bought them for you.'

'I thought …' And then he came forward and took her in his arms. 'You didn't call.' She hit her fist against his chest.

'I tried. I was cut off. You know the exchange. I did try.' He held her at arm's length now and looked at her. 'I missed you, you know.'

'I need a tissue.' Her nose was running.

'So the jacket's not your colour then?' He wiped her cheeks. 'You could try it on.'

It fitted perfectly. He must have asked Maria for measurements.

'Thank you. I just got a fright, that's all.'

'I've been thinking about you all the way back in the car.' He started to sing, 'Your lips, your smile, your sweet embrace.' He held her close and danced her round the room. 'Where's Maria? I brought her something too.' He let go of her and walked over to his suitcase that lay opened by the door. Just then Maria appeared. She had a strange knack of doing this, almost on cue. Tom handed her a pint bottle with liquid in it from his suitcase. 'Sea water. Just what you asked for.' Maria held the bottle up and scrutinised the floating bits in it.

Maria had known that Tom was going to the sea. Catherine watched her.

'God knows what she does with it,' Tom laughed. 'I need something a bit stiffer. Won't you pour me some whisky and I'll get changed. I'm exhausted. I've been driving all day.' He was already halfway down the passage on his way to change. She could feel his restless energy unsettling the air in the house. He had another life, out there, away from the farm where she didn't know what he did. Catherine turned to ask Maria why she hadn't told her that Tom had gone to the sea, but Maria had disappeared to her room with the bottle of sea water.

When Tom came back Catherine handed him a drink and they sat down. 'So tell me what you've been doing. I saw your painting. It's very good,' he said.

'You like it? You don't think the water in the pool is wrong.'

'No.'

'I tried to get Maria to swim, but she told me she was cold. Did you get your business done?' She didn't want to talk about his wife.

'Yes.' He was stirring his ice with his finger. 'Won't you play me something on the piano?'

She ignored this and tried to change the conversation.

'I went riding all the way along the river. Ptolomy has been eating too many oats. He nearly threw me off. And we planted a garden at the school.' She could hear herself jabbering on nervously – trying to keep things light.

'Play me something,' he said again.

'I've forgotten how. I never learnt things off by heart.'

'It doesn't matter. Make it up as you go along. Play me to sleep.' He closed his eyes.

So she sat down and lifted the lid of the piano. It had been so long. At first she played notes that were discordant, but he didn't move, didn't flinch. And then she made herself forget him. The last time she had played was when her mother was dying.

'Katie, play for me,' her mother had called from her bed, but her voice was a whisper and her face was gaunt. She had wanted to leave her body so badly. 'Play to me, you play so well, take me somewhere else. Come on Katie. Take me back there to the veld, to the river. Take me up in the koppies. Take me to the church.'

Her fingers moved on the keys and she felt something rising up inside. Something she'd kept carefully sealed. She was crying. She stopped playing and closed the lid of the piano.

When she passed Tom to go and sit down, he put his hand behind her thighs and pulled her towards him. He stood up. 'I want to kiss you.' His mouth tasted of whisky. He was holding her and she leaned against him. His body was warm.

'I'm tired.' She moved away. 'I'll see you in the morning.' It had been too much of a shock, she couldn't go to bed with him, not again, not so fast.

In her room she took all the clothes out of her drawers, refolded them and put them back in. *My things.* She lined up her three pairs of shoes under the bed. *My shoes, my room, my house.*

Catherine went outside onto the driveway and Maria joined her. They didn't say anything – just lay down and looked up at the sky. Maria had the bottle of sea water next to her.

Tom watched them from the window: two women, two girls. He could see that there was nobody else. They were alone in a world of their own. 'What do you want?' He remembered her voice. I want what is yours. I want to stay here, he thought. He looked at their fingers touching in the dust as they lay on the driveway. 'I want to tell you the truth, but it's too late now; I've gone too far. I can't leave now.'

Eleven

Hendrik ran through the veld, leaping over a branch that crossed the path and shouting up into the sky. He spun around and did a flying leap; his bag bounced against his chest. Catherine was going to love the sketches he had done, and when he could use colour there would be an explosion. There were flowers all along the path and he stopped to pick some – five pink and five white. He knew that she liked them because before, when he had taken them to the church, he had heard delighted laughter.

The next time he'd been in the church the flowers had been joined by their stems to make a chain and there were small fingerprints in the dust.

Today he had his bathing costume on underneath his shorts so that he could just leap into the water when Catherine went swimming. He could jump from the ledge and show her how to do a back flip and he would ask her if he could draw her.

When he got to the pool she wasn't there yet, but he was early. He took out the bottle of wine and put it in the water to cool. Then he sat on the bank and drew a pattern in the earth and decorated it with pebbles. She was late. He took off his clothes and jumped in the water, diving down as deep as he could go; holding his breath for as long as he could. Then he got out and lay on the rocks to dry. She had been held up. But she would be here, he knew. He wanted to be busy when she arrived and he took out his pad and started to draw the pool.

*

Catherine and Tom drove in silence. Halfway along the road a hare came flying out of the bushes in front of the car. There was no way Tom could have stopped; there was a car coming in the opposite direction. He would have killed them both – so he hit the hare. Catherine looked back to see its back legs still flapping helplessly as it lay there on the road. Tom pulled over and they got out. She watched as he went over and wrung its neck. It was so quick. 'Are you all right?' he said, coming back and taking her hand. 'There was nothing I could have done.'

'I know, it was the best thing. Tom?' But he didn't seem to have heard her. They got back in the car.

'I've had the plane fixed. There was a problem with the freeplay on the joystick. Willy took her up the other day. She's perfect now. I'll give you your first flying lesson. In an aeroplane, that is. I reckon you go flying all the time in that head of yours.' He was fiddling with the radio.

They flew for hours; further than they had been before, tracing the river down the valley and over the edge of the escarpment where the land fell away, into the opal hills that led down towards Lourenço Marques.

*

Hendrik heard the aeroplane before he saw it. Catherine was up there with Tom, flying. She had forgotten. How could he have thought? Would she see him if she looked down? He stopped sketching, crumpled up the drawing, and threw it into the water where it swirled round and was carried over the rocks and down the river. It would have been perfect, but then Mr Fyncham had come back and messed it up. Hendrik took a handful of stones and threw them as hard as he could against the cliff on the other side of the pool. He had been so stupid, to let himself feel like this, to open his heart. He sat down, lit a cigarette and started to drink.

He didn't stop drinking until he had finished the bottle of wine. Then he got up and stumbled up the path from the pool.

Maria passed him on the path outside the church, but he didn't look up. She saw the tears streaking down his face.

*

On the way back to Hebron, Catherine drove. She turned off the tar road, but instead of going down the hill to Hebron, she drove along a dirt track that led to a waterfall on the edge of the escarpment. They had seen it from the air. Tom had never been there and she wanted to show him how spectacular it was. She drove as far as she could, then they got out and walked. The water plummeted over the edge of flat rocks down into the krantz far below. They sat, dangling their legs over the edge. She could feel the spray as it blew back up.

'There are leopards down there in caves.' She pointed at the steep sides of the krantz.

Tom had brought a bottle of wine from the car and he opened it. They sat swigging from the bottle. She lay back on the rocks. He traced his finger over her calf. 'Unhand me sir, for I am not a boy.' She didn't know why she had said it. It was so good to have him back.

'You are crazy, aren't you?' His hand was warm on her skin.

'It's what the groom says to the dashing rake in those romantic novels when she reveals that she is not actually a boy and that she desires him.'

'I can't say I read romantic fiction.'

'Pity. Lilly can't get enough of it. It's her secret passion.'

Tom was pulling her skirt off, pushing her shirt up. She felt his tongue on her skin, licking her stomach, and the sun burning them, and then they were pulling off their clothes in a mad urgency and laughing at their frenzy. Whose leg was whose, whose tongue, whose skin?

She felt the cold fine spray off the waterfall and the salty taste of his sweat and then he held her hands above her head and she squeezed his fingers and the rock scratched her back. She wrapped her legs around him and he pushed inside her and she shouted up into the sky and he held her head between his hands and looked at her and loved her, she could feel it. She could feel the plants growing around them and the cracks in the rock and the water.

She stared at the clouds above her, drifting across the sky. Tom had fallen asleep and she had put his shirt over his head to stop his face from burning.

'Will you take me with you?' She had said it aloud.

He opened his eyes at the sound of her voice. 'What was that?' His voice was sleepy.

'When you go away again. Will you take me with you?' She traced a piece of grass over his arm.

'I'll take you. I promise.' He turned to face her. 'You make me happy, Miss King.'

Twelve

Two weeks had passed since Hendrik had gone to the river pool to meet Catherine only to find that she had forgotten him. He had stopped going there, he had stopped going to the church.

His mother was sitting with Nettie de Vries and Ella. They were having coffee and biscuits. He could hear them from where he sat.

'He's gone. Tom Fyncham's gone.'

'How do you know?'

'He was supposed to collect feed from the railway siding on Thursday but he didn't arrive, so Davel took the feed up to the house at Hebron. The native girl said he was gone.'

'And I saw her on the road up to Hebron – the King girl. She was just walking, but it didn't look like she knew where she was going. I stopped and asked her if she was okay. She didn't even greet me.'

'The native girl didn't tell Davel when Mr Fyncham would be back. She just watched as he off-loaded the sacks of feed. Didn't help. Just stood there. And the King girl – she was standing behind her in the doorway – Davel says she didn't have shoes on. Her hair was all messy, like she hadn't brushed it for days.'

So Mr Fyncham had left Catherine, he had left the farm. A spark ignited in Hendrik's heart. She would need help on the farm and he knew what to do. He knew all there was to know. Soon he would go over to Hebron, but not immediately, he would wait to make sure before he went over to offer his help.

They ate supper early, as usual. Hendrik's mother asked him why he was so quiet. No reason, he told her. She didn't repeat the conversation she had had with Nettie and she didn't know that he had overheard them speaking. She wouldn't want him to know that Tom Fyncham had left Catherine alone at the house, but she must know that he would find out sooner or later, the way that news travelled. 'How is Dirk?' she asked him.

'Fine.'

Then his father discussed farm things with him and told him how he had had to deliver a calf while Hendrik was at school. It was a breech birth. He'd had to stick his arm into the cow and turn the calf around. The calf had lived. It had been a wonderful thing.

His mother's mood was light too. She suggested they go on a family holiday after Hendrik had finished his exams, to the sea. They hadn't been on a holiday together for so long. It would be a celebration.

Hendrik half listened as his mother described places she had visited in the past with his father when they had first been married. She told him about how they had met at a dance. For the first time for a long time, he saw a look of genuine affection pass between his parents when his father reached over the table and took his mother's hand.

He would take Catherine a gift of some sort, he thought as he lay on his bed after supper. He stared out of the window, across the veld to the ridge. It was so beautiful out there in the dark. Whenever he lay on his bed, he wanted to be outside under the stars, up on those huge boulders that attracted the lightning. There was iron in those rocks. They looked as though they had been hurled from a height and shattered on impact with the earth, and rolled down the hill, finding their resting place. And then the plants had grown in and around them. Sometimes he wondered if there was a God up there, in the sky, and if he had thrown them in anger or if they had slipped from his hand, or if he'd tossed them joyfully, like dice and then watched as they had split open.

He had to go tonight, he couldn't lie in bed and wait; he would never sleep. He put on a clean shirt and trousers and packed his bag with cigarettes and half a bottle of whisky that he kept in his cupboard. The whisky would steady his nerves. Then he opened the window and jumped down onto the driveway and was off into the dark.

Hendrik stopped on the way to Hebron, in the church, to look at Catherine's picture. And then he was off again, running down the path past the river pool and out onto the avenue of gum trees. The whisky had given him courage. He wouldn't lurk in the shadows watching the house; he would walk boldly up the stairs and knock on the door.

But he didn't have to knock. The door was open, as were the windows in the rooms at the front of the house. They were flung open to the warm night. Music was playing. He had come to associate it with the house. It sounded gay and light. But when he got inside he could sense that something was wrong.

The only light on was a lamp in the sitting room. It took him a while to make out a figure sitting in an armchair in the corner. Catherine didn't move when he crossed the carpet. The record came to an end and the needle scratched backwards and forwards. Hendrik went over and lifted the record off the turntable, because Catherine wasn't going to. He approached her cautiously. She didn't seem surprised to see him; she was too drunk.

Her face looked smudged as though someone had taken a photo of her but it was out of focus, the muscles in her face had gone slack. Then he saw the cut on her forehead and that it was still bleeding.

'It's okay.' He put his hand out. She stood up slowly, holding onto the chair.

'No,' she shook her head. 'It's not okay.' A look of annoyance passed across her face.

'Why are you here? Where's Maria?' She tried to walk towards the door and he held out a hand to steady her.

'You have a cut. You should put something on it.' But she wasn't listening to him.

'Did you see her when you came?' They reached the door and she let go of his hand and walked unsteadily out onto the stoep where she sat down on the wall. 'We had a fight.' She was not really talking to him, but to herself. 'She said I had no right to shout at her. I shouted at her.'

*

She had been mad, crazy with frustration and disbelief.

'Why didn't you come and find me when Tom left?' she had screamed at Maria. 'You knew he was leaving, you must have known. I was at the school; you must have seen him packing. Did he tell you to give me the note?'

And Maria had replied in an injured voice. 'I was out. Don't shout like that. I wasn't at the house. I was at my mother's. What can I have done to stop him?'

'You just don't want Tom here,' she had accused Maria. 'You want it to be just the two of us. But I love him.'

'I'm leaving.'

'Where are you going?'

'I don't know. But I'm not staying and listening to you screaming at me.'

'You can't go.'

But Maria had. She had just walked off into the dark leaving Catherine alone in the house.

*

'Did Maria do that?' Hendrik pointed to the cut on Catherine's forehead. This time she looked at him with something close to anger, as if to say, how could he think that. He felt out of his depth again with her. He didn't know what to do. He had never seen her like this.

'I fell and cut myself. But I'm not worried about that. Maria has gone.'

'I'm sure she'll come back.' He tried to sound reassuring.

'Do you think so?' She stood up and went back into the house, this time more steadily as though she had composed herself. 'Do you want a drink?' she asked him, already pouring a glass. 'I've been drinking all evening. Tom has gone, he promised he would take me with him. All he left me was a note just like the last time. It's the second time he's left. He left a note and he said this time would be the last time but that's what he said last time.' Her voice sounded flat. She was tired. 'Why don't you choose a record. Put it on. Maybe the music will get her to come back.'

He went over and looked through the selection. He saw the jacket sleeve – Edmundo Ross's Latin American Big Band and put the record on. The singer sang in a foreign language he couldn't understand. He sat next to Catherine for a while, in silence, until he could think of something to say that didn't sound stupid.

'I waited for you by the pool. I brought the sketches.'

She looked at him and for the first time that evening, he felt, registered that he was there, a separate person, in the room with her. 'I'm sorry.' She was biting her lip. 'I've been forgetting everything. I'm sorry. That was unforgivable. Do you want to dance? Let's dance.' She stood up shakily.

'I don't know how. I'm afraid I …'

'Don't be afraid. There's nothing to it. I'll show you.' She wanted to lean against someone.

And she did. Soon he was dancing with her. He had a good sense of rhythm, she told him. He just enjoyed holding her, the closeness of her. He could smell her hair and her skin. At the end of the song he didn't want to let her go. He felt he should do something, that she was expecting something, he should kiss her. But then she pulled away.

'Can you hear something?'

'Do you want me to go and look for her?' he asked.

'She could be anywhere.' She shook her head. 'No, that would make it worse. We had a fight. No, stay here with me. If you don't mind. I don't want to be alone.'

He went to fetch her some water in the kitchen when she complained that her head hurt.

'Tom's gone away. He didn't take me with him.' She said it bluntly; she was sobering up. 'The phone rang and I answered it – I shouldn't have answered. It was her, Isobel, Tom's wife. I know it was. Now she knows I'm here.'

'I'll stay here with you.'

'I need to sleep now. You could sit out here.'

But when she started along the passage she stumbled and he had to help her down to her room and onto her bed. He pulled the sheet up over her.

'Will you stay until I fall asleep?' she asked.

'Of course.'

'Thank you.' She closed her eyes.

*

Maria saw the strange boy leaving the house. It was late. She had come back to say she was sorry. The boy passed her by the gate, his head down, walking fast. She didn't greet him.

When she got back to the house, Maria found Catherine asleep in Tom's bed – out cold.

*

Maria had been in the church after Catherine had fought with her.

She had just wanted to sleep there, on the floor. But they hadn't let her.

The dark room kept coming back and there were three people there. The woman with the silver clasp, the man and someone else. Someone who was in trouble. Someone who was sick.

Thirteen

Maria opened the curtain and Catherine groaned and covered her face. Her mouth was dry and her head was pounding. 'What are you smiling at?' She sat up, annoyed at Maria. 'Are you satisfied now? I was alone. I got drunk.'

'Alone?'

'I don't remember. I smashed a vase. I don't remember.'

'The boy was here.'

'What boy?'

'The Afrikaans boy. The strange one.'

Catherine remembered his face more like a dream than flesh and blood. And that she had felt safe. But she couldn't remember the details and she had a horrible feeling. 'What did I do? Did I do anything?'

'I don't know. I wasn't here. I saw him leaving.'

'When was that?'

'This morning.'

'Why didn't you come inside?'

'I don't know. I fell asleep out there.'

Catherine sat up in bed, but it made her head worse. 'Won't you get me some pain killers? I'm sorry about the fight,' she added. Maria brought her a glass of water and the pills.

When Catherine had taken them Maria told her what she had seen. 'It's in the studio. You'd better go and look.'

'What is it?'

It was a sheet of paper, one of her sheets, and the boy had pinned it up on the easel for her to look at. It was a charcoal sketch of her, lying naked on her bed. It was beautiful but she took it down and tore it in half.

She stood in the shower. The anger twisted itself into a knot in her stomach again, every time she thought of Tom leaving. She had planned to go into town with him to shop that afternoon. It had been hard to concentrate at school. How could she teach multiplication when all she could think of was Tom inside her? She had finished school late and run the last bit up to the house, hoping he wouldn't be too impatient because she still needed to change. But when she had got to the house she found that he had gone. There was a note. It was the last time, he had promised. He was looking forward to flying with her soon. He was sorry. He would phone.

But there had been a week and no phonecalls. Then she had exploded.

'Do you think you're the only one who's ever been in love?' Maria had accused her.

The icy water shocked Catherine back from some dazed place she'd been in for days. She towelled herself dry and pulled on a summer dress. Then she went to get coffee in the kitchen. Maria had squeezed orange juice. 'I'm going to find him,' she told her. 'It's no use me staying here going crazy. I am panicking every day now. I have to do something. I don't care what he thinks. I need to know. I feel strong enough now. I don't care if I have to leave.'

'But you don't know where he is.'

'There must be something. I just have to look through his things.' And she remembered the pansy shell.

It took her the whole morning before she found a card that had slipped down the side of his desk. She held it up like a trophy in front of Maria.

There was an address of a hotel on the card and a sketch of a palm tree. It was enough to go on. She wasn't frightened now. She had got her courage back, she could face them.

⋆

Catherine is driving down through the opal hills on her way to Lourenço Marques. She has the postcard with the name of the hotel on the dashboard. She puts her foot down, the window is open and the hot air rushes in. She drives too fast around the bends, but then the road straightens out, stretching out in a shimmering line to the horizon. The bush flashes past, the red rock face, the thorn trees, the air is humming. A bird of prey circles in the pewter sky. The mountains fold like wrinkled skin back into the earth. She is descending a steep mountain pass into the lowveld. The land falls away on either side into gorges full of trees. A troop of baboons sits on the side of the road scratching themselves in the sun. At the bottom, where the land opens up again, there is a tearoom. She stops. The engine is hot from driving fast. Her hair is full of dust. She goes to the toilets and washes the dust off her face and hands. She looks in the mirror. Her face is golden from the sun.

Outside she sits on a wrought-iron chair under the trees. Everything is slow here, even breathing is slow. The waitress takes her time before she comes to serve Catherine.

'A toasted cheese sandwich and coffee,' she tells the waitress. She needs to keep awake. When the sandwich comes, the cheese is too hot to eat. There is a column of ants moving in formation across the faded red and white cloth on the table. She watches. The waitress comes over.

'Is everything okay?' she asks. She is curious, so is the man at the next table.

'Fine,' Catherine assures her, but the waitress hovers, reluctant to go. 'Aren't you scared of travelling alone? What if you get a puncture?' She warns Catherine that there is a roadblock near the border. The police are looking for blacks – there's been trouble. There is an underground movement, communists, weapons. As she talks she looks down at the concrete slabs under her feet as if they are actually down there tunnelling away. 'The police found weapons,' she says, 'they were smuggled across the border.'

The man joins in. 'No, it isn't safe,' he says. 'How far are you going?'

The waitress brings her another coffee. She thinks of Hebron. Cut off from this, from news, from the rest of the world, from how other people go on. She thinks of Maria's ghosts that live under the house; they have their own strange underground movement.

She gets out her map and starts to trace her route to the coast with a pencil. Inside the café she can hear the shrill voice of the waitress. 'You kaffirs are so clumsy. Look what you've done. Now you've broken it.'

Catherine watches the scene inside the tearoom with a strange detachment. The black woman has knocked over a box of straws. 'Now look what you've done. Pick them up!'

'Sorry, Madam.' The woman bends down and starts to pick the straws up one by one and put them back in the box. Catherine thinks of Maria.

She checks the oil and the water and fills up with petrol. Then she is driving again. The radio is playing dance music. Maria would like it. Maybe she can buy her some records at the coast.

She arrives at the border post and gets out of the car to have a cigarette. The man from the café comes over.

'Are you all right?' he asks her.

'I'm fine.'

'I'm also going to Lourenço Marques – I've got an aunt there. I'll keep an eye out for you on the road.'

An old black man walks up to them. He has been sitting with a woman on the ground under the tree watching them talking. His face is old and shrunken. He holds a rusty jam tin in his hand. There is a plant growing out of it. Around his arm hang strings of beads – they are strung-together seedpods, brown and orange and grey.

'Five bob,' he holds out his arm, displaying the necklaces. 'Choose one, Madam.' The necklaces are threaded together with fishing line. 'Magic beans,' he says. He lifts the plant out of the tin and shows her the roots. A seed is forming in amongst the white threads, a small heart shape. He puts a necklace around Catherine's neck. She hands him five bob. Maria would have bargained him down. She would have robbed him blind.

'How does it look?' she turns to the man from the café, but he has walked away, embarrassed that she had bought something from a native.

The land is flat across the border. After an hour of driving she loses track of time. She is in a trance – the road the sky, the sky the road, the road the sky. She puts her hand out of the window and opens her fingers. The radio station is picking up music from LM.

★

Maria scratched out squares in the dirt driveway at Hebron. She picked up a pebble, threw it, and jumped. It had been a long time since she had played hopscotch. She wanted to play, she didn't want to think, she didn't want to sleep. Two butterflies flew around her head as she jumped up and down the squares she had scratched. She looked up – it was a sign. Katie was wrong, there were signs, they were all around you if you cared to look. Her hair was a messy frizz – her braids had come out and she had lost her comb.

She was unravelling, casting herself out like fishing line on the river. Perhaps someone would reel her in.

One night, lying in the dark in the tin church, she had seen golden lights. They had run through thin tubes from her toes and fingers through her body and out the top of her head. She had felt a wind rushing through her spine and she had grown a tail, her vertebrae shooting down between her legs. She was running in a cheetah's body across the open plains, the golden grass under her feet. All movement. A small hand on her forehead, a warm sweet breath in her ear, laughter. Back at the house at Hebron she had gone to look in the mirror in the bathroom and seen the cheetah's dark tear marks on her face – old eyes that saw from the beginning to the end.

She was bored with hopscotch now and she went to lie among the flowers in the garden. She breathed in the smell of honey and pulled up her dress to feel the warm air between her legs, soaking in the sun like a lizard. Then she felt a stab of pain. Catherine had been there like her heartbeat. Now she was gone and there was someone else standing in the garden with her. She could feel them.

★

Catherine drives slowly along the beachfront in LM. It is mid-afternoon. She has made good time. She finds the hotel without too much trouble. It is set back from the road. There is a garden with pepper trees that go down to the water's edge. An avocado tree overshadows the tables outside in the courtyard. An avocado pear has fallen from the low branches and lies split open on a wrought-iron table underneath.

'It's a sign,' Catherine can hear Maria's voice.

She thinks everything is a sign – good or bad, depending on her mood. She carries the image of Maria with her as something to hold on to.

She gets out the car and walks up the path. A young couple are sitting at one of the tables. A radio is playing somewhere inside. She looks for Tom's car, but can't see it anywhere.

'Good afternoon,' the couple greet her as she walks past.

The reception desk is in the entrance hall. Behind the desk is an archway leading into a small sitting room furnished in heavy materials. There are photographs on the walls and a passage that leads through the hotel out into a sunny courtyard at the back filled with pot plants and small concrete statues. A parrot is sitting in a cage squawking. She rings the bell on the desk.

A man comes through from the sitting room. He has a florid, soft face and a gold ring on his finger. She would say that he was in his forties. His skin is tanned and wrinkled on his chest from too much sun, and he smells strongly of aftershave. 'I'd like to book …'

'You're English.' He seems delighted by this. 'Single, or double?' His tone is confiding.

'Single – do you have a room with a view of the bay?'

'I only have one at the back. It looks into the courtyard. It's quieter there though. Things can get a little rowdy, if you're not used to noise.' He says it knowingly. 'Just the one suitcase?' He has come around from behind the counter and picked up her suitcase. 'Light! You're not staying long?' Then he claps his hand over his mouth. 'I'm sorry. I'm prying. It's human interest, isn't it? Life can get – well, never mind my problems. If you'll follow me.'

He leads her upstairs. There are plants all the way along the passage, red lilies; it is like a greenhouse. Perhaps that is the musty smell. The carpets in the passage get wet and don't quite dry. He opens the door to the room. It is small and shabby but clean. He puts the suitcase down on the bed. 'We serve breakfast from 8 until 9. Would you like coffee or tea?'

'Tea, thank you.'

'I'm afraid we don't do dinner but I can recommend places to eat. I have some brochures downstairs. You might like to do a tour? I'm Malcolm, by the way,' he introduces himself. 'Rather late than never,' he laughs.

She is tired now and wonders why she came.

'Did someone recommend us?' He's at the door. 'It's just that it's a small establishment, and you seem to have come a long way.'

'Yes, a friend. He's stayed here before.' Catherine hesitates. 'Do you own the hotel?'

'Oh, no. I just manage here. No, the owner lives downstairs – there's an apartment off the reception. Her husband left her some time ago. She …' but he decides not to say what he was about to, perhaps an indiscretion. 'Well, let me not keep you, you must be tired.' He closes the door softly behind him.

She lies down on the bed, listening to the parrot scratching in the gravel at the bottom of its cage and falls asleep.

*

Maria opened her eyes. The Afrikaans boy was standing a few feet away. She sat up and waited for him to speak. She enjoyed his awkwardness. It was her house now that Tom and Catherine were away and she wouldn't let him in. 'You came to see Miss King,' she said finally.

'Yes.'

'She doesn't remember anything of last night.'

'Is she here?'

'She's gone down to the coast with Mr Fyncham.' She picked a flower and twirled it around in her fingers. 'I'm going to join them – we are all going on holiday at the coast.'

'I came to collect something, from Miss King's studio.' Hendrik waited.

'The house is locked. You can't go in.'

'Do you know when she'll be back?'

Maria shook her head. 'It's no use waiting. I won't let you in.' He turned to go. 'You should be careful,' she called after him.

*

When Catherine wakes up it is dusk. She goes down to the reception and rings the bell and waits, but no one comes. There are brochures lying on the coffee table through the archway in the sitting room, behind the reception desk. One of the brochures that she leafs through has a map of the city in it. There is a list of restaurants and someone has circled one with a red pen. It's on the beachfront, not far from the hotel.

The tide is out. She passes an elderly couple walking their dog. The woman could have the man on a leash too, the way he trails after her. She looks at the man's face. She looks at every man who passes but none resembles Tom. A young couple passes. The girl leans into the boy; he turns and kisses her.

Tom is here somewhere. She can see the restaurant ahead.

The air is humid; fruit bats fly in the trees on the verge of the beach. There are still fishermen in the water. They are pulling in their nets.

The waiter at the door of the restaurant takes her coat and ushers her to the bar.

'I'll have a whisky,' she tells the barman. There is a window facing out onto the water and she sits in front of it, watching the boats bobbing up and down, drinking her whisky too fast.

A woman comes into the restaurant and the waiter shows her to a table, for two, by the window, next to Catherine's.

She says something in Portuguese to the waiter and he laughs. The woman's hair is dark and she is wearing red lipstick and a green dress that clings to her body. Catherine stares at her.

She should get up now, go back to the car and drive back to Hebron. But she can't. The waiter brings the woman a glass of wine, and adjusts the table settings.

Then Catherine hears a man's voice behind her. 'Single malt.'

She hears ice hitting the glass and then he is walking towards her but she doesn't turn round. She can feel him getting closer. He passes her and sits down opposite the woman at the next table, takes her hand and kisses it. They laugh.

It isn't Tom.

*

Fourteen

Catherine wakes up in the early morning. The air is already hot. She switches on the fan and watches the blades as they whir round and round. She is in a strange hotel at the coast, but there is a feeling of familiarity. She is looking for Tom. She is not in her dream – she is really here. There is already the sound of cooking going on downstairs, the clattering of dishes. Catherine gets up and walks down the passage to the shared bathroom. Only a trickle of water comes out of the shower and what water does come out is a rusty colour. The mosquitoes hover in clusters around the showerhead. She feels grimy and the shower doesn't help much. She will have to swim.

Malcolm, the manager, meets her in the foyer. He is holding a small fan, like flamenco dancer's, and is fanning himself. Someone, a woman, is shouting from a room nearby.

'Sometimes I don't know why I live here, why I put up with her.' He stops. 'Did you have a pleasant evening? Where did you eat?' He holds her wrist as he ushers her out to a seat on the verandah. 'Coffee or tea?' He clicks his fingers and a black waiter wearing a grubby fez appears to take her order. Malcolm has to dash, his employer is calling him again; there will be trouble if he ignores her for too long.

The young kissing couple at the next table keep looking at her and then speaking in low tones. They are disturbed by the fact that she is a single woman.

'Would you like to join us?' they ask her.

'No, really. I'm fine,' she assures them.

Malcolm is back. This time he sits down next to her. 'You have plans for today? There's a ferry ride or you'd like to swim?' Catherine takes a chance.

'I'm meeting someone,' she offers.

'Of course you are. I knew … well that sorts that out.' He is embarrassed. She is looking at him too directly perhaps. She fishes in her bag and brings out her cigarettes and offers him one. 'I won't say no.'

'Perhaps you know the person I am meeting,' she says carefully. 'He's stayed here before.'

'Try me.'

'His name is Tom Fyncham.' She watches his face carefully. He hesitates before he answers – perhaps out of a loyalty to clients.

'I'm afraid I'm quite new here. He might have come before I took over as manager.' He is smiling reassuringly now. Someone was calling him. 'I'm so sorry I have to go. We could have tea later. I'd love to chat – hear news from the outside world if you know what I mean. Why don't we meet here at four?'

It is impossible to find Tom here. She takes a bus along the coast to a beach.

The water is warm. She lies on her back and floats. This is where Tom is. Drinking in bars, eating in restaurants, walking along the beach, swimming in this sea.

Catherine stretches her arms out; the sun is burning her face and she dives underwater. It's so quiet underneath. She has hired a snorkel and goggles and flippers from someone with a stall on the beach. He offered to come with her but she told him that she would be fine alone.

She dives down. Small fish dart between the coral; yellow and black and orange. As she surfaces she feels the sun beating down on her head and she swims back to the shore and returns the snorkel and goggles. Then she changes into her dress and catches the bus back to LM. The ferry is filling up with passengers. She sits in the front, away from the smell of the diesel engine.

When the passengers disembark across the bay she is the last to get off. She has no plan. She will just wander around. There are only a few houses and they look expensive. The roads are wide with big areas of green bush on the verges. A dog comes to a fence and barks at her. Some children are swimming in a pool, jumping in and out of the water.

At the end of a cul-de-sac she stops in front of a wrought-iron gate. There is a house that must have spectacular views across the bay. But it has been abandoned, or else badly neglected. The grass has grown long on the lawn, and the swimming pool is empty and cracked. She thinks of the postcard, and her dream. There are leaves floating in a puddle of stagnant water at the bottom. A cat slinks past. There is a dead bird on the verge of the road and the ants are making a trail around it.

She feels a melancholy here and turns to go back past the children swimming. Too much time alone, she tells herself. They would both go mad, she and Maria. She needs to be in a bustle, around normal people with jobs – who take holidays by the sea – and she heads back to the ferry and walks along the shore. She has to wait for the return trip, and finds a bench to sit on.

A family are having a picnic. The children's voices remind her of teaching and she feels on safe ground again. They are building a sandcastle. They wave at her and she waves back. 'Come see.' They practise their English. She goes and admires the castle and helps them build a moat.

'You like it here?' the mother smiles. 'On holiday?'

'Yes.'

When she gets back to the hotel everyone is still having a siesta except for the couple who are kissing on the grass. They don't notice her at all.

The room behind the reception area, where she has arranged to meet Malcolm is small and crowded with heavy furniture. It makes the air thick and cloying. It reminds her of Mrs Coombe's house, only that house was cool inside, this is hot although the fan is on. She feels strangely detached, she has all day.

If someone besides Malcolm comes in she will say that she came to read the brochures. There is a pile of them on the coffee table in the centre of the room and she opens one so that she won't be caught out. A woman's shawl hangs on the back of the chair she is sitting in. Directly in front of her on the wall is a calendar with the days ticked off on it. Somebody has been counting them. Underneath it, in a glass cabinet, is a statue of the Virgin Mary and some plastic flowers lying on the table. There is an English newspaper with the crossword half done. Catherine looks at the missing clues.

Down: Dare

Across: Reticent

It must be Malcolm who gets the paper, she thinks. In the corner of the room there is a door which leads into Malcolm's quarters and the rooms where the owner lives. She can hear someone moving around behind the door, but it doesn't open.

She picks up the paper again. She thinks she might as well try the missing clues in the crossword while she waits. It is then that she sees the photograph album that has been half-hidden under the paper and magazines.

Afterwards she will think that if she hadn't lifted the paper up, or if a certain magazine hadn't fallen to the floor, she would never have found the album and never have been tempted to look inside – and what she discovered might have remained hidden.

But she does open the album.

⋆

At Hebron Maria wakes up with a start from where she has been sleeping in the yard under the peach tree.

⋆

At first Catherine doesn't recognise anything in the album. There are old sepia snapshots of a man in military uniform standing very upright in front of a door. The next picture shows him with a woman with dark hair tied back in a bun. She turns the page and finds pictures of a rock pool and a sea urchin. She thinks of her mother's prints of the rocks, the sky, the water. When she turns the next page she recognises what she is looking at. It is the fortress from her dream and the postcard on Mrs Coombe's wall. There is the sea washing the steps and the palm tree in the centre of the fortress.

She looks around the room. The door is shut but she can still hear someone moving around. Out of the window the sun is shining and beyond the garden the bay is like a milky pond. She feels numb; she can't feel her hands or feet. She tells herself that she can close the album and leave the hotel and drive home. She wishes she had never found the card with the address of the hotel on it. But she keeps turning the pages and she knows what she will find, as though she has been through this album before, many times. There is a photograph of her father standing on a beach. He is older than she remembers. His trousers are rolled up so that he doesn't get them wet and he's wearing a white shirt rolled up at the sleeves. He is walking away from the camera, holding the hand of a little girl. The girl is wearing a bathing costume with a frill around the waist. Her legs are thin. Her hair is long, black and straight. It isn't her – it isn't Katie.

Take my hand, I'll race you to the sea.
I want you to run Dad, run.
Okay. But don't fall. Hold on tight.
Faster – run faster.

The door opens. Catherine doesn't have time to close the album. She looks up in confusion. 'I was just …'

'It's okay.' Malcolm leans over her shoulder. 'I've always wanted to look at them, but the boss doesn't like it.' He takes the album from her and looks more closely at the girl with the dark hair. 'She looks sweet, doesn't she?' but Catherine can't answer. 'Are you alright? You look pale.'

'I feel dizzy.'

'Too much sun – it's very strong. I'll get you some water.' His tone is confiding. He has put the album back down on the table and is pouring her a glass of water from a bottle on the side table. She wants to rip the photograph up into tiny pieces and burn them all.

'Is this here?' She points to the photograph of the beach.

'Looks like it.' He hands her the water.

'And this house?' She points to the photograph next to it.

'I'm sorry, I don't know. My boss doesn't like me looking through her things; she caught me once.'

It is the house that she found at the end of the cul-de-sac. But in this photograph the swimming pool is full, there is a gardener mowing the lawn and there are chairs and a table next to the pool. A woman is sitting with her head bent so that Catherine can't see her face, only the top of her wide hat.

There is a coughing sound and Catherine turns to the door. An elderly woman has come into the room. She has grey hair tied back in a bun. She stops when she sees Catherine and turns to Malcolm for an explanation.

'*Quem é ela*?' she asks him.

'A guest,' he shouts.

'This is my boss.' He rolls his eyes at Catherine. 'She's going deaf.'

The woman says something else in Portuguese.

'She's looking at the album. The photographs.' Malcolm explains. The woman comes closer. She frowns.

'I was looking at the girl on the beach. She's pretty.' Catherine holds the album up so that the woman can see which picture she is talking about.

'That's Isobel,' she snorts. 'She hasn't been to visit me for month now, look.' She points to a calendar on the wall where the days are crossed off. 'What kind of daughter is that?' Then she looks at the album again. 'And that man,' she points to Katie's father, 'he left us.'

Catherine turns the pages of the album – it is something to do with her hands, but she wants to reach the end of the album, she needs to get past the photographs of her father and of Isobel. And there on the last page – there she is – staring out. Katie.

Catherine looks at the photograph of herself, aged eight, pulling a face, sticking her tongue behind the gap in her teeth. There is a dark blur at the edge of the picture where Maria had tried to stick her hand in front of Katie's face. 'Who is this?' Catherine points to the image of her as a child.

'That girl,' the woman sighs, 'that's Katie – she's dead.'

Fifteen

'What is it, Hendrik? What's wrong?' They were sitting at the table eating lunch. Hendrik had been in his room since he came back from Hebron and his mother was worried. Hendrik kept thinking of what the native girl had said. Catherine had gone away to be with Tom. The maid cleared away their soup bowls. 'You've been so distracted. Hasn't he?' His mother turned to her husband, but he had opened the paper and was reading something. 'The exams are coming up. Nettie says that Dirk has started studying every night.' She brushed some crumbs off the table into her hand. 'Perhaps I should be doing more to help you. If there's anything I can do, you will let me know, seun?'

'Ma, it's fine. I'm okay. Don't worry.'

'I can't help it.' She cut them each a slice of trifle. Hendrik wasn't hungry. He'd lost his appetite. 'Just a small piece.'

'Ma, I can't.'

'What's wrong? You haven't been eating properly. And you need to. You need energy to study. Nettie says Dirk can't get enough food.'

'Dirk's greedy. He always was.'

'It's healthy.' He watched as she poured the cream over the trifle and started to eat her pudding. His leg was tapping under the table. He couldn't relax, it was driving him crazy – this sitting around in the house waiting and the constant chatter.

She had finished her pudding. His father had been eating while he read the paper. It annoyed his mother so, she wanted them to be all together as a family at dinner times. To talk. But their family wasn't like that. 'Elise didn't see you at school on Friday, or Thursday.' She was trying to make it sound light, because she knew how he hated what he called her prying. But it was concern. She wanted what was best for him.

Hendrik thought of Elise sitting in the back of the classroom staring out of the window to the vacant plots of land between the houses – just scrub growing, waiting for something to be built on it. Vacant is what the boys called Elise; Hendrik had told them to shut up several times. 'Elise is always dreaming, Ma. She doesn't notice. You know that.'

'But she told Nettie.'

He moved the placemat around.

'Hendrik, we're worried about you.' And now she looked directly at him and he could see what anxiety he was causing her.

'Who is we?' he asked. Not his father. He was reading the sports pages now.

'Nettie and me. You haven't been yourself.'

He knew where this was leading – that was the worst thing – he always knew what she was going to say and then she said it. By the silence and his mother's concentration on picking the cherries out of her trifle, he thought that she had decided not to, but then she looked up and his heart sank. For a moment he had hoped. 'You haven't been over to Hebron, have you? You haven't been painting at the house?'

'No, Ma.' He managed to control his voice.

'Because it's not safe. Nettie's girl saw that black girl from Hebron up in the trees by that native church.' She could see that he was interested now. 'Evidently she was lying on the ground. Her legs were jerking and her arms, she was talking nonsense and there was spit, you know, foam at her mouth. It gave the girl such a fright. Nettie had to give her sweet tea to calm her down.'

'Epileptic fit.' His father looked up from the paper. He had been half listening. But this was something of interest, worth commenting on. 'Cattle are getting fits too in that camp by the river. Might be something in the water.'

'Do you think it's the water?' His mother was alarmed now that it touched on her world. 'Do you think we should be boiling it?'

'It's not in the water, Ma.'

'But she was moaning and speaking in some different language, the girl told Nettie. There was something very wrong.'

'You have to put a stick in their mouths or they swallow their tongues.' His father turned, folded the paper up, and reached for the coffee pot.

Hendrik stood up and started to stack the pudding bowls. He had to leave the room. 'The girl can do that. I know you've got work to do.'

'I'm going out, Ma.'

'But I thought tomorrow was the first exam?'

'Let him go. It's Sunday.' His father winked at Hendrik, he was on his side. It was unexpected.

'Will you be back for supper?' Hendrik didn't answer.

*

There is a chain around the gate of the house in the cul-de-sac – the house in the photograph. Catherine looks across the overgrown lawn. An upstairs window is open. She has come to confront them. She has to.

She had been the last passenger to board the ferry; people had stared at her as she steadied herself against the rail. Somebody had asked if she was sick, if they could help, and she had told them that it was the smell of the diesel. Someone had offered her a Coca-Cola. Earlier, when she fled the hotel, she had been sick. She had retched in the bushes. There was no church to run to, no Maria here. She was on her own in this strange place. Malcolm had come out after her. He had suggested that she lie down, but she had said then that she had been feeling dizzy all day – that what she needed was fresh air and to walk. He was puzzled, but he let her go. As soon as he was out of sight and she was on the beach she began to run. She ran and ran as if she could physically run away from it – run out of herself. Disappear. Then she had seen the ferry about to leave.

'I've got some unfinished business.' She hears Tom's voice in her head. 'I can tell you everything when I get back. Do you like prawns? I want to take you all the places I've been. I've got some business.' There are other voices, all slurring together. 'You must watch these rust spots, rust is the death of cars. Do you love her? It's not like that, it's complicated.'

'You must be Catherine King. How do you know? The painting inside, I'll show you.' Her breath is shallow now. 'I'll take you flying. What do you like?' She tried to push the panic down and still the voices. 'Tell me the things you like. Three sugars for your tea. Don't answer the telephone. Leave it. Why so many questions?'

There is no bell to ring at the gate and there are spikes on top. It will be difficult to climb over. She pulls the chain. To her surprise it slides open under her fingers and the gate opens when she pushes against it. She is inside standing on the overgrown driveway. Nothing happens, no dogs bark to scare her off, no one shouts at her. On the way up to the house she passes the empty pool. When she gets close to it, she can see that the pattern on the tiles is of peacocks. Someone's hat has fallen to the bottom and lies in a crumpled heap on the bottom, faded by the sun. There is a prickly pear tree in the bushes and bougainvillea that has gone mad all around the house. The curtains are half-open in the downstairs windows and she looks into a large room with high ceilings and dust covers over the furniture, for painting, or moving, in or out, she wonders.

She knocks on the door and waits – but Tom doesn't answer it, nobody does. There had been water in the swimming pool once, and parties and noise and laughter.

She knocks again and then opens the door. The entrance hall is empty, the air is cool inside because of the tiles on the floor and the thickness of the walls. There are a few boxes, lying unopened and a brush and pan. A shutter bangs at the back but no one comes and she starts to climb the stairs that lead up from the hallway, listening for footsteps all the way. Upstairs there is a corridor with rooms leading off it. She has done this before, trespassed in a house where she was uninvited.

'I'm going to Mrs Coombe's house. I'm going to see what's in her room.'

'What if she's there?'

'Then I won't go in of course. Sometimes you can be stupid, Maria.'

'What will you do if she comes when you're in the room?'

'I'll hide. I'll say I got lost.'

'Lost?'

'Alright. I'll think of something.'

'What if he's there? Mr Coombe?'

'I'll say I've brought a message from my mother – a thank you card – for the dinner.'

'Have you got one?'

'No. It doesn't matter. I won't get caught. Do you dare me?'

'Only if you bring something back. To prove that you've been there.'

'Like what?'

'Creams or something, or jewellery.'

There is a single bed in the first room. It has a dust cover over it. Apart from that the room is empty. From the window Catherine can see the back garden that leads down to the sea. A small dinghy is bobbing up and down on its moorings at the end of a jetty. There is garden furniture under a wild fig tree, overlooking the sea, but leaves have covered it too, and wild figs have fallen and rotted on the ground. Tickbirds are pecking at the fruit. With binoculars, from here, someone would be able to see the beach on the other side of the bay. They could even see the outline of the hotel. They would have been able to see her walking on the beach and swimming or retching into the bushes. They could watch the ferry, carrying passengers back and forth.

The stillness in the house makes it difficult for Catherine to move for fear of making a noise. She walks down the passage, looking into the rest of the rooms. Three of them haven't been used – they are empty. But someone has been into the bathroom. A towel has been dropped on the floor and there is a tube of toothpaste and a toothbrush and a comb. She picks up the towel, walks to the end of the passage, and opens the door.

Tom's things are folded on the bed. She recognises his shirts and trousers lying next to a map that is spread out on the bed, which hasn't been made, not properly, the sheet has just been pulled up over the pillow and there are no blankets. But it is hot at night here. The mosquito net is tied in a knot above the bed. Under the window is a small desk. Someone has emptied a bag on it and there are papers lying scattered in a mess. Catherine folds the towel she has carried from the bathroom and puts it on the bed. Then she picks up the shirt and starts to fold it and refold it. It is no use. She feels numb inside. She knows she needs to cry, but she can't and she lies down on the bed. She can smell him on the pillow. She lies there for a long time listening for footsteps, or the sound of a door opening, unable to move. All she has to reassure her is Maria's voice in her head.

'What would you do if someone came in the house to kill you?'

'They won't, that's stupid, Maria.'

'But what if they did?'

'I'd climb out of the window. I'd hide up a tree. People are stupid, they run in the open and then get caught; I'd climb up a tree and watch and wait till they were gone. What would you do?'

'The same.'

Someone is in the house now; she can hear them moving about downstairs. It is a woman, by the sound of the footsteps. Perhaps Isobel has come to meet Tom here. Tom. It doesn't really matter now. Nothing does. When Catherine can hear the footsteps in the passage outside Tom's room she gets up and moves to the window.

She gathers up the papers on the desk and puts them in her bag, not knowing what she is doing. It's a reflex, she doesn't think. Then she goes out into the passage.

The woman holds her hand over her mouth in fright when she sees Catherine. They stand and stare at each other.

She is black and she is wearing a maid's apron. She's come to clean. 'I was looking for Mr Fyncham.' Catherine explains, trying to sound as calm as she can. The woman seems relieved.

'Engleesh,' she shakes her head. 'Mr Fyncham no here.'

'Mrs Fyncham, Isobel?'

She shakes her head again. 'Mr and Mees Fyncham no here.'

'Do you know where they've gone?'

'No. Clean,' she says and holds up the broom.

The woman follows Catherine down the stairs. At the door she stops. 'Car?' The woman is wondering how she has got there.

'I walked,' Catherine explains, 'from the ferry. Are they coming back?' But the woman doesn't understand.

Catherine is halfway down the drive when the woman calls after her. She turns around and walks back. The woman taps her chest and says. 'Evangelina.'

'Catherine. Catherine King.'

'King. Yes.' Her face lights up as if now she understands. 'Santa Maria.' The woman is searching for a word; she shakes her head. 'Santa Maria.' She says the name over again.

'Mr King is at Santa Maria?'

The woman smiles and nods.

'*Sim, sim*. Santa Maria.' Then she bends down and draws a cross in the earth with her finger.

'Mr King is at Santa Maria?'

'*Sim*, Santa Maria,' the woman nods, happy to be understood.

'*Onde é* … Santa Maria?' Catherine can't remember the words. But the woman just repeats the name.

When she gets off the ferry Catherine turns to the man next to her. 'Do you speak English?'

'*Un pouco* – a little.' He smiles, his eyes light up.
'Santa Maria. *Onde é* Santa Maria?'
'Ah. You go up this street. Turn left.'
'Left at the stop sign?'
'Yes.'
'Is it far?'
'Not far. I show you.'
They pass a stall selling fruit and vegetables. When they reach a small cobbled square the man stops and points.
'There,' he says, triumphantly. 'Church of Santa Maria.'

*

Hendrik went inside the church. Maria was asleep on the floor at the front. It was silent inside – not even a sigh. When he went closer he saw the earth on her dress and the muddy marks on the floor where she must have dragged herself across from the door. He squatted down beside her. He could see her eyes moving under her eyelids. She looked drugged. He took his sketchbook out of his bag and fanned her face. He had brought water too, if she needed it. Slowly her eyes opened and she began to focus. She tried to say something but he couldn't make sense of it. Then she turned to look over her shoulder. 'Katie?' she said it clearly. He took her wrist and felt her pulse. They had done first aid at school. Her heart was beating, but slowly. He shook her and for an instant her eyes opened again. He took his water bottle out and wet her lips with his fingers, then he helped her to sit up against the corrugated iron wall.
'Where's Catherine?' she asked him, and tried to stand up.
'You need to rest.' She closed her eyes and didn't struggle again. He studied her face. He had never looked at her like this, she had always been so aggressive with him. Now that she wasn't cursing him, or warning him, he saw how pretty she was, how smooth her skin was, and the shape of her eyes. She took his hand.
'How long have I been here?' she asked.
He shook his head.
'I slept?' She looked confused.

'You had a fit.' He handed her the water so that she could drink again. 'You should see the doctor. Miss King must take you into town to the clinic.'

She was shaking her head. 'I don't need a doctor.'

'Has it happened before?'

Then she started to cry. It was so unexpected, Hendrik didn't know what to do. He searched in his pockets for a tissue. He had a piece with charcoal stains on it and he handed it to her. 'It will be okay.' He put his fingers gingerly on her shoulder but she seemed not to notice him.

'I have to go now.' She got up. 'I have to get back to Hebron in case they come home.'

Determinedly Maria crossed the camp, taking the short cut up to Hebron. She made her feet move, one in front of the other until she reached the house. Gabriel shouted at her from the stable, but she ignored him. The house was just as she had left it and she went inside and made herself a boiled egg. She needed to eat. She would be no use if she fainted. After lunch she took a blanket out into the yard. It was what she had done before, when things went wrong.

She sat down with her legs out in front of her in the shade of the peach tree. And then she started to cry again because Katie couldn't. Because she knew that she had found out, but not everything – not what they had done in that dark room. And now Maria knew, she had seen it in the church – Isobel and Tom standing in the dark.

Maria must have fallen asleep from exhaustion. When she woke up she heard noises in the driveway. She heard a jazz tune playing and smelt the heat off the engine as a car drew to a halt outside the house.

Sixteen

The church is cool and dark inside. Catherine waits by the thick, carved wooden door until her eyes adjust and she can make out the interior. There are stained-glass windows. The altar has an embroidered cloth spread over it. In one corner there is a confessional and at the front, to the side of the altar, there is a table with candles burning on it. An old woman is kneeling in the front pew praying. Catherine looks for Tom. Why would he be in here? The maid had said that *they* had gone. The numbness is wearing off now. *Mr and Mrs Fyncham have gone.* Gone where? To Hebron? And she imagines Isobel sitting next to Tom, holding his hand under the table and talking to her father, the same father who had held her hand and walked on the beach, the same father as Katie's who had played in the sea, carried her on his shoulders, shown her the rabbit in the moon?

Catherine's father had sat down and drunk whisky with Tom. They had laughed about something together – some shared joke. He had shown Tom where his farm was on the map. Isobel had leant over and touched Tom's arm. 'We can go there. We can farm – you'd like that, wouldn't you?' and then she'd turned to her father, Katie's father, and he'd told them about the river and the store and the church on the ridge – all the places to see. He'd told Tom that he could make money there. He'd told Tom about his family who had left. What had he told him about his daughter, Katie?

Catherine walks to the front of the church and sits down in the pew on the other side of the aisle from the woman. As she looks up at the altar she thinks of Maria's vision in the tin church, but there is nothing up there that she can see. Nothing that can help her. She has never prayed inside a church. What they did in the tin church was not praying. They had sung the songs with the congregation and closed their eyes when they knelt and their lips had moved. Whispering nothings; that's what Maria called it. As long as your lips are moving they think you're praying. She wants to think of Maria – she needs to hear her voice.

'What if they can read lips? What if they know we're not praying?'

'But they can't tell you because that means they had their eyes open and weren't praying either.'

'Very clever.'

Maria is pleased.

The old woman gets up, makes the sign of the cross and leaves the church. Nobody comes in for a while and then a woman and her daughter come in and pray, and then go to the front to light a candle. A candle for a blessing – for a wish.

'Maria. We need sand.'

'For what?'

'To stand the candles in.'

'What about earth?'

'I suppose.'

They scoop it into a bucket and fight over who is going to carry it up the hill.

'Now what?'

'We need to put it in something.'

'The baptismal font.'

'It's like chocolate pudding in a big bowl. Pity it doesn't taste like chocolate.'

'Where the candles?'

'Under the altar, in a box.'

'What if the priest see?'

'We can clear up afterwards.'

'Okay. Now we stick the candles in the earth.'

They push them down until they stand without falling.

'Now what?'

'Now we light one.'

'You've got to make a wish when you light your candle. Say a prayer.'

'You ask for something?'

'Yes.'

'Do we ask for same thing?'

'Yes.'

'Like for boyfriend?'

'We don't want boyfriends.' Katie's tone is stern.

Maria frowns.

'Like books to read then?' She tries again.

'We have books.'

'You have books.'

Catherine looks at her. 'You can have my books.'

'Your mother she won't let me. She'll think I steal them.'

'No. We must wish for something that we can see if it comes true. We need proof.'

'Like a miracle. Like sea coming apart? Like the burning bush.'

'Yes.'

'We can wish that tonight church will light up in the dark.'

'Tonight.'

Maria lights a match. The flame burns down towards her fingers.

'See how long you can let it burn without blowing it out'.

'Why?'

'I dare you.'

They stand there burning matches down, singeing their fingers.

And then they remember what they are supposed to be doing and they light the candles. One each.

Later at Hebron, when the stars are out, Katie jumps out of the window and runs out onto the driveway. Maria is there too, waiting.

The church is blazing in the dark. It's their miracle.

Catherine gets up and moves to the small door at the side of the church which leads out into the graveyard at the back.

There are lots of tombstones. It will take her a long time to search for her father's grave. Some of the stones are very old – it won't be among these. Some of the graves have got beautiful flowers on them, lilies and roses, and someone has come and cut the grass around them. Catherine thinks of Maria putting tobacco and bread on her lover's grave. She had seen her sitting there on his tombstone, rocking in the dark. Maria thought she didn't know.

At the far side of the graveyard is a row of graves that look more recent and she crosses between the stones to read the names on these tombstones.

But she can't find her father's name. A man is digging a new grave but he can't understand her when she asks who it is for. She goes down the rows again. She can feel the panic rising now as she reads off the names and dates. They spin around her head making her dizzy and she can't breathe. Born, died, born died, 1896–1939, 1900–1930, 1940–1945 – a child. Perhaps she has the wrong church, but there is no one she can talk to who knows anything. The dates slur and shriek at her.

Seventeen

Catherine's legs are stiff from driving and she is dusty and sweaty. She hasn't stopped, since the border. She pulls off the road onto the veld, on the hill above the farm. There is a track through the grass to an outcrop of rocks. She climbs up the rocks and sits. The roof at Hebron is visible from here as it lies between the trees and the church. The sun is setting and long shadows fall across the land. It is lonely up here. She watches the women making their way along the dirt road with sacks of wood on their heads, their hips swaying with the movement. Some of the women have babies tied to their backs with blankets, arms against their backs, the rhythm rocking them to sleep. Children run ahead laughing or arguing. They are going back to make a fire and cook supper and go to sleep under a blanket in the smoke.

Then she opens her bag and takes the papers out – the papers she has taken from Tom's house. She couldn't look at them before, not in that strange place.

Most of them are bills and she crumples them and puts them back in her bag but amongst them is a shopping list. It's written in black ink. She holds it up in the fading light. The thick dark strokes cut across the paper – meat, bread, potatoes, gin …

Catherine stares at the letters. She has a paper with letters and words formed like this, she has kept it in the bottom of her suitcase, but she doesn't need to read it to remember the words, they are imprinted on her mind:

I am writing this letter as a friend of Mr King's to send my condolences on your father's death … I am sorry to inform you that he was deeply in debt when he died. All he had, had to be sold to rectify this. All I can send you is his watch.

The letter had been unsigned. She had read it again and again until it had become real. Now she runs her fingers across the words on the list – written with the same ink. And at the bottom, where the list ends she has written:

Tom, could you buy these when you are in town. Thank you.
Isobel

Catherine tears the list up into tiny pieces and throws it into the wind. She rubs her arms and stays out until she is cold. Then she gets up and walks back to the car.

There are two cars in the driveway at Hebron. One is Tom's. He has come separately from Isobel then.

Catherine has decided to leave the farm. Maria can come with her if she wants to – she won't want to stay now that Isobel and Tom are in the house. She will take Maria to the coast, or inland, to the city.

She walks slowly up the stairs, stopping before she opens the door.

Books have been hurled to the floor along with ornaments; two vases have been smashed and one of the windows onto the courtyard is cracked. Records lie in a heap next to the gramophone. Someone has taken her clothes and strewn them across the carpet.

There is violence in the room now, just as there had been before.

'Stop it.'

She can hear her father's voice, and her mother's.

'Why should I? Tell me why I should. How could you?'

'Not in front of Katie and Lilly.'

'It's a bit late for that.'

'We can sort this out.'

'No we can't. We can't bloody well sort this out.'

The vase crashes to the floor. A piece catches her father on his face. There is blood.

Lilly is whimpering.

'Shut up, Lilly.' Katie screams.

They turn and look at her.

'Katie, it's not your fault. I'm sorry,' Dad says.

'Do you think that makes it alright, saying you're sorry?' Her mum hits him.

'Yes, Mum. Yes it does.' She wants them to listen. But they don't hear her.

'I'm taking them with me.' Her Mum is wild.

'You can't do that.'

'Yes, I can. You won't stop me.'

'Have you asked them? Go on, ask them.'

'Do you want to go with me, or do you want to stay here with your father?' she asks them as if it's as easy as choosing blue or red mugs. They stare at her. Lilly starts to cry again. 'It's not fair. That isn't fair to ask them.'

Katie runs out of the room, onto the stoep and stares out into the dark.

'Shut up!' she shouts. 'Just shut up all of you.'

'Maria!'

Catherine walks around the house looking in all the rooms. She sees where her cupboard drawer has been yanked open. There are clothes across the floor. She goes out into the courtyard. The slates are still warm from the hot stillness of the day.

Catherine, tell me what you like, and don't say mangoes. You're beautiful, you know that, don't you.

'Maria!'

In the dusk, the colours on the walls are soft, her brush is still lying next to a can of paint where she has been painting the mural. The prickly pears are nearly ripe enough to eat.

One or two have fallen onto the slates.

You know, up here I can forget everything.

What do you want to forget?

'Maria!' Catherine stands outside her door and calls, but she isn't there. The house is silent. She tries Maria's door but it is locked. She didn't even know that there were keys to the doors in the house. In the kitchen she finds a half-chopped onion on the chopping board. Something is burning in a pot on the stove. There is smoke everywhere. She takes a cloth and moves the pot.

If there's trouble we'll meet in the church. I'll wait for you there. Whoever gets there first must wait.

It's beginning to get dark as she reaches the school building. Some of the children are still working in the garden behind the school. They run up to greet her. 'Where you been?' they ask her. 'Where you going?'

She calls them by their Swazi names and it makes them laugh. She tells them to go home, it's going to rain, it's too late for them to be out. 'Go on, shoo.' She chases them, and they shriek with laughter. She feels strangely calm now, disconnected from herself.

'Where you going?' they ask her again.

'Up to the church.'

'Is too far, you'll get lost.'

'I know the way.'

'One and one is two. Two and two is four,' they shout after her.

She wants to be their age again – going up the path with Maria.

'Let's sing a song.'

'Why?'

'For courage. That way we won't be scared in the dark.'

'Are you scared?'

'No.'

'I am.'

'Okay. I am a bit. But nothing is different from the day. It's just that someone has switched the light off.'

'But people can do things in the dark without you seeing them.'

'But we know this path.'

'Yes. We must have been a hundred times.'

'A hundred trillion, billion times.'

'What's that sound?'

'Just a cow.'

'Let's go back.'

'We can't. Not now.'

'We'll sing a song. Down by the bramble bushes
Down by the sea

Come on, sing!'

'Boom boom boom
True love for you, my darling
True love for me
When we get married ...' they sing together.

'I can't see in the dark. What are we going to do up in the church?'

'We've got to see what is up there at night.'

'The light?'

'Yes.'

'But that was a miracle.' Maria runs ahead.

'I know, but it ...'

'What?'

'It might not have been one.'

Maria stops and turns back to face her. 'What do you mean?'

At the fork in the path Catherine stops. She listens. There is a rustling in the grasses, of a small night creature, and the distant rumble of thunder, a frog down by the pool, the wind in the reeds and another sound – a sound coming from the river pool. She can't go on. She steps back and squats down in the grasses.

She doesn't want to see anymore. She will sit and wait for Maria to find her.

★

Maria sits on the grave behind the church and hugs her knees to her chest. She watches the lightning streak across the sky like blue electric snakes and thinks of Catherine. She wants her to come home – and not come home – at the same time. She doesn't want her to see what happened in the house and what is happening in the river pool. She will keep it a secret from Katie, she has to. This time it will be her secret only, not to be shared or spoken about. It will be her secret, buried under stones, the grass growing over it until even the place where it was buried is forgotten deep inside her, under the rocks. It will crumble to dust and one day the river will wash the dust away and it will be lost forever.

She will think of Katie, she will remember her in the dark.

'You can't tell anyone what we saw. Do you hear, Maria?'

'But I didn't see. Katie, I didn't see, you wouldn't let me look through the window. What did you see in the church?'

'Nothing. It's a secret.'

'You lying. You see something, otherwise you give me leg up so I can see. We make a wish to be friends.'

'So?'

'Friends tell each other secrets.'

'They wouldn't be secrets then.'

'But we have secrets. You say you always tell me.'

'I've changed my mind.'

'You can't change your mind.'

'Look, it's raining cats and dogs.'

'I hope they can swim like us, not drown.'

'I wonder what drowning is like.'

'It don't hurt.'

'How do you know, Maria?'

'Let's slide down on our bums in the mud.'

'We can wash our dresses in the pool.'

Maria knows what drowning is like. She counts the time between the thunder and the lightning. The storm is still a way off. She thought she was drowning when the Afrikaans boy found her in the church. She couldn't remember how she had got there, only that she had fallen in amongst the trees. But she remembered what she had seen.

She closes her eyes and feels the air. She can't see the pool but she knows what is happening down there. She had seen it when the boy had found her in the church.

Coffins floating on the rivers of rain that washed down from the church, through the trees and over the edge, down into the pool. Her dead aunt whooping as she rode her coffin between the trees. She was holding a pair of reins as if her coffin were a horse. Her clothes were tatters and she had a hungry look in her eyes. Not far behind came another coffin. A little girl's coffin. Behind her bobbing and swirling in the water was a goat. Its stomach was bloated and it stared at her with yellow glassy eyes.

A whole carnival was riding down from the church. She searched through the water for Katie. She called her, but she couldn't hear because the singing was too loud. Then she saw another face appear from under the water and two hands, scrabbling to hold onto a log that was floating past. It was a woman. Her hair was wet and sticking to her scalp. Her white hands were clawing the air. Maria watched as she went under. She didn't try to help her.

Maria gets up and goes inside the church. She will wait there for Catherine. It is the only safe place.

★

Hendrik sees Maria go into the church. He is watching from the trees above the pool. When she is inside he turns back and moves to the edge of the trees and looks down through the branches at the pool. He watches as Tom Fyncham lifts Mrs Fyncham in his arms and carries her out of the water to the side of the pool. Mr Fyncham lays her down on the ground, then he stands up, turns his back on her and walks away into the dark.

In that moment Hendrik knows what he has to do. He feels like he did when he watched Catherine sleeping and when he had to shoot the cow that had broken its neck. He has to hide Mrs Fyncham's body. He has to dig it deep under the earth so that Catherine will never see it. It is her pool; it is her farm. The dead woman didn't belong here. Catherine must never find her, she must never know or she would leave the farm.

And then he thinks practically, he knows that he needs a spade and a sack and that he will have to ride back to the farm and that there isn't much time, because Mr Fyncham might come back. It starts to rain heavily as he turns and runs between the trees, past the church, down the koppie to where his horse is waiting, tied to a tree, shying in the storm. And as he rides he prays that he won't be too late when he gets back.

*

Catherine crouches in the grass at the edge of the path. The sound at the pool has stopped and now she can hear footsteps coming towards her. She is soaked and she moves back further from the path, into the long grass. When Tom passes her, all she can make out is his shape in the dark. He is walking slowly but steadily away from the pool, not running in the rain. She knows that the noise at the pool was him – that strange sobbing sound. He passes so close to her that she could reach out and touch him, but something stops her. She's not safe out here alone. She needs to go to the church and find Maria. When Tom has gone she stands up. She doesn't want to go further but she makes herself. Where the path forks, she chooses the one that goes down to the pool. She has to know what is there before she goes to the church.

Isobel's skin is pale in the moonlight and her hair is sticking to her skull. Catherine looks down at her. Isobel – she says her name. She wants to put her hand against the woman's face but she can't. Her eyes are shut – Tom must have shut them. She is dead.

What happened here? On one side of her head there is a gash and the blood has congealed around it matting the hair together.

She has been hit once, very hard, or perhaps many times.

She should be covered, not left with this summer dress wet and clinging to her body. All Catherine can think of is that she must be cold, that she needs to be warm. But there isn't a blanket to put over her. Perhaps Tom has gone for a blanket. But she is dead.

Where had Tom been going? To the house. To call the police – but he wouldn't do that. What would he do? Would he leave, without a note, with no explanation like he had before? A note to say what: that he had killed her – that it was an accident.

Catherine is so tired she just needs to sleep, to rest. She turns and pushes on through the rain, up the path to the church.

Eighteen

Maria is sitting with her back to the door and a blanket wrapped around her. Catherine wonders how long she has been waiting in the church. She knows that Maria saw what happened in the pool. She stands at the back and watches her. Maria doesn't turn around. Perhaps she is asleep sitting up, perhaps she is in the middle of some vast roaring ocean. The moonlight is flooding the church – it is a pool of silvery grey light, shimmering on the wood. The pews are rocking on the water.

Catherine needs to remember. She needs to see their faces, to hear them laughing.

'Don't go into the church.'

'Why?'

'Not yet. We must look through the windows first to see who's there.'

'To see light.'

'Yes.'

'I need to make a pee.' Maria squats on the ground.

'So pee.'

'What if it scary?'

'It won't be scary.'

'What if it the priest?'

'He's asleep in bed.'

'How do you know?'

'What if it a criminal, hiding and he got a knife and he wait for us?'

The window's too high to look in. They made them high so that children can't look in.

'Give me a leg up.'
'What about me?'
'You can go afterwards.'

Maria helps her up so that she can see through the window.
There is a paraffin lamp on the altar.
Katie catches her breath.

There is something spread out on the floor and stuck to the walls of the church – small squares. Someone is sitting on the floor in the middle of the squares. She has her back to the window. Her hair reaches halfway down her back. She is singing – a faint sound.

Catherine tells Maria to keep holding her up, just a second, two seconds more. They are not squares, they are pictures – photographs. Of the rocks, the river, the sky, the sea, shells, insects. Her mother has stuck them on the walls and spread them out around her on the floor in the church. When she turns for an instant and looks up towards the window Katie can see the tears on her face.

Catherine lets go and falls onto the ground on top of Maria.

'What is it? Who is it?' Maria gets up and tries to jump to see in the window.

'Nobody.'

'But I can hear they singing. It's the lady who sings.'

'Nobody's in there.'

'Why are you crying? What's the light?'

'It must be a miracle.'

'Why are you crying?'

'No reason. Because … just because.' She gets up and starts to run back down the path.

'Wait for me,' Maria calls after her. She catches Katie by the pool.

'I don't get chance to see. I go back.' Maria makes as if to run back up the hill.

Katie stops her.

'No.'

'Why not?'
'Don't go up there.'
'Why you can't tell me?'
'It's a secret. My secret.'

Catherine walks across the floor to where Maria is sitting. Maria turns at the sound of her feet. 'I thought you'd got lost.' Maria stands up and hugs her friend.

'Maria, she's dead. What are we going to do? Her head was smashed.'

'Did he see you? Tom, did he see?'

'No. I was in the grass, he walked past me. It must have been an accident Maria.'

'What if it wasn't?'

'It was.'

'How do you know?'

Catherine doesn't answer the question. 'What are we going to do?'

'Nothing. We must stay here. It's safe.'

'We can't stay here forever.'

'When it's light we'll go down.'

Catherine sits down next to Maria with her back against the altar. It's dark outside. The thunder is crashing.

'What did you see?' Maria asks. 'Down at the coast. What did you find?'

'I found that hotel, the one on the card.' Catherine picks up one of the old hymn books that has been left forgotten under the front pew and starts to page through it. She needs something to do with her hands, she doesn't have her cigarettes.

'What else?'

'I found a photograph album in the hotel. There were pictures in it.'

Maria takes her hand.

'There were pictures of Isobel and my father – her father.'

'It's okay now.' Maria squeezes her hand.

‘Did you see anything else?’

‘No.’ Catherine turns to look at her. ‘Did you know? Did you see?’

‘Not for a long time. But then I saw.’

It is too late for Maria to hide what she has seen.

‘What did you see?’

‘There was a room. It was dark. Isobel and Tom were together.’

The door of the church bangs open, the rain is coming in now.

‘Your father was in that room too. He was sick.’ Maria hesitates – she thinks she hears the sound of small feet pattering on the floor, and small hands pulling at her dress.

‘I want to know.’ Catherine is shivering.

‘Isobel was writing something. Tom didn’t want her to.’

‘But he didn’t stop her?’

Maria shakes her head.

‘She made him write his name on that paper.’

‘Tom?’

‘No, your father.’ She hears their voices sigh; she feels their small fingers on her head, and Catherine feels them too. ‘With that paper she took away the farm.’

‘But he signed it – he signed the paper? He wrote his name?’

‘He was sick. It was dark.’

Maria watches Catherine. ‘It’s going to be okay now,’ she says.

‘She hated me.’

‘Yes. That thing inside ate her up.’

‘But why didn’t Tom tell me?’

‘Perhaps he loves you – perhaps he is a coward.’ Maria puts her arm around Catherine and pulls her closer. ‘Perhaps he knows you won’t love him if he does.’ Maria starts to draw patterns in the dust on the floor.

‘What will happen to Isobel? She’s out there in the rain. I saw her, Maria, she looked so cold.’

Maria is silent for a while, then she tells Catherine.

‘She’ll disappear. She’ll be washed away. Gone. Never coming back.’

'You can't just make her disappear. You can't just make it better for me always.'

Maria unwraps the blanket from her body and covers them both with it. They lie side by side on the floor.

'What if he's at the house when we get back?'

'Will you talk to him?'

'What if I don't want to? What if he killed her?'

'Do you think that?'

They have painted mud on their bodies at the pool. It has dried and is making their skins feel tight. They run up to the church carrying their dresses. It's midday. They drop their dresses at the door.

'Have you got a pin?' Katie asks.

'Why do we need pin?' Maria frowns.

'To make our fingers bleed of course. Or a knife.'

'Do we have to cut?'

'Yes. To make it work. It's like the initiates. They do things like this at mountain school.'

'Sometimes girls go too.'

'Here, I've got a knife. Put your finger out.'

'No.'

'Okay. I'll do mine first.'

'Ow! It hurt?'

'Not much.'

'I'll do yours now.'

'No, I do my own.'

Katie watches as Maria scratches her skin.

'You have to go deeper. Here.'

'Ouch!'

'Okay. Now we mix the blood.'

'And then?'

'We say something to keep us together. Always.'

'Always.'

They laugh, scared at what they have done and said. Then they run out into the sunshine.

When the sun comes up Catherine wakes up. Her face is wet and Maria tells her that she was crying in her sleep. They walk down between the trees and down through the rocks to the pool. Isobel's body is gone.

Tom is waiting on the stoep at Hebron. Catherine sees the pain on his face, the tiredness, he has been up all night. She wants to touch him, but she can't. He gets up and comes towards her.

'No,' she says.

Maria goes inside the house but she sits just inside the door watching.

'Where have you been?' he asks Catherine.

'I went to the hotel.' Catherine can't look at him. 'I found out, Tom. I went to the pool last night.' She can hear the children laughing and chatting as they walk down the dirt road to the school. They will be expecting her to come and teach them reading and about plants and animals. She has to say it. 'Did you kill her?' She can feel the rage inside him now. He grabs her arm.

'You tell me Catherine. Look at me.'

But she can't look at him. 'I don't know, do I?' she says. 'You lied to me.'

He gestures, but she won't let him speak. She is shaking she is so angry now.

'Don't worry I won't call the police. I don't want them on my farm. It is my farm, isn't it Tom?'

'It's always been your farm.'

'I don't want them walking on it, asking questions, interrogating Maria. People will want to blame her – they are frightened of her, they don't understand.'

Maria sees Tom wanting to tell Catherine, to explain, but Catherine turns away from him.

'I don't want to know,' she has her back to him, 'I don't want to know anything anymore. I just want you to leave my farm. It's over.'

She goes into the house and closes the door.

Nineteen

'Mr Fyncham's gone for good this time.'

'There must have been a fight. I wonder what happened at the house.'

'Well, she's still there – the King girl and that native girl.'

'He chose his wife after all. They all do you know. They have affairs but they won't leave the wife.'

Nettie smoothed the tablecloth and patted at the edge of her mouth with a napkin.

'Davel heard Miss King at the store – inquiring about cattle prices. She wants to sell some of the stock. She hasn't got any money.'

Hendrik had read the same sentence ten times. He was sitting outside but the window behind him was open and he could hear their conversation as clearly as if he had been sitting with them round the table. He shut his book.

'Has Hendrik heard anything?' It was Nettie.

'No.' He imagined his mother shaking her head. He knew what she was about to say. 'He's been very stressed lately.'

'It's the exams. Elise has been nervous too.'

'I keep telling him to take some of my nerve tonic.'

There is an unusual silence between them at the table. Then Nettie gets up. Hendrik can hear her chair scraping on the floor. She walks to the window. He can hear her breathing – she struggles to fill her lungs because of her asthma. 'You know that storm the other night?' She has turned to look at his mother.

'Well, Mrs Venter told me that the rain caused a mudslide. All the earth on the slope above their house just washed down – it came as high as the windows – destroyed the flowerbeds. She says the house is filthy. She says she can't cope anymore. Her husband doesn't lift a finger to help.'

It had been a week now and Hendrik hadn't been back to check that the stones that he had put over the place where he had buried Mrs Fyncham hadn't rolled off, or the rain hadn't exposed the body. When he thought about it, he was shocked by what he had done.

That night he had got back to the pool to find Mrs Fyncham's body still lying there – and no sign of Mr Fyncham. He remembered how Isobel's head had bounced on the rocks when he had dragged her up the hill. He had had to sling her over his shoulder like a bag of mealie meal. He had told himself over and over that she was just a dead thing, like the plants or rocks – that her spirit had gone. She was just bones and blood and fat and skin. Afterwards he had had to burn his shirt because it was stained with blood.

At school he hasn't been able to concentrate on his work. Every time the door of the classroom opened, something jumped inside him. One morning a police car pulled up in front of the school. Hendrik watched out of the window as the policemen got out and walked to the front of the building. It would only be a matter of time before they were in the headmaster's office and they sent for him. He had waited but nothing had happened. The bell for break rang and everyone ran out into the quad, into the sun. He had stayed sitting in his desk in the classroom.

He would wait another week, he told himself, before he went to Hebron to offer to help Catherine. He had seen her crossing the street in town, collecting supplies, but she hadn't seen him and he hadn't called out to her. The weather was changing and the grass would start to turn colour soon. They had had the last storm of the summer. He had been to the pool, but the water was too cold for her now – she hadn't been back there. The nights were getting longer and in a few months they would need to light fires in the evening.

His father had seen Catherine down at the store buying feed. If she was going to sell stock, did she know which ones to sell? Hendrik could help her. Someone should tell her that she should be moving the cattle to the winter camp – perhaps the boys on the farm would see to it.

She was working all day now, out in the veld. They were mending fences on Hebron. He had seen her out riding when it was getting dark. It was as if she didn't want to go back to the house. One night he walked past the house and saw her sitting outside on the stoep as she had done with Tom, drinking whisky and smoking a cigarette. She was tired. He could sense it.

Nettie was leaving. Hendrik heard them getting up. His mother had come out of the house to wave her off. They watched as she got into her car and ground the gears. 'She's such a terrible driver,' his mother laughed as she watched her friend nearly reverse into the wall. Nettie waved gaily out of the window and took off in a cloud of dust. 'How are you?' his mother turned to him.

'I'm fine, Ma. Don't worry.'

He couldn't remember how deep he had dug the grave. Perhaps he should have taken Mrs Fyncham's ring off, but that would have been wrong too. It was just that after some time, if something happened, if someone found her, and identified her … He had heard stories of wild animals uncovering bones in graveyards as they searched for prey.

'Hendrik, Nettie says Elise is also having trouble with her nerves. She bought some of that tonic for her. If you …'

'Ma, I don't need tonic.'

'Where are you going?'

'I'll be back for supper. I'll see if I can find some mushrooms in the veld for you.' He didn't wait for an answer; he was off down the path. It was good to be running again, he could feel the blood pumping around his body and his tension easing.

He found the stones as he had left them, on top of the grave; nothing had been disturbed. The sun was shining directly on the boulders, warming them. He took his shirt off so that he could feel it on his back. He loved that feeling of the cold gusts of wind and then the warmth on his skin when the wind passed as he sat on the ledge dangling his feet over the edge. He lit a cigarette and pulled the smoke into his lungs. This was better than his mother's nerve tonic. 'Have you got a cigarette? I've run out.' He remembered Catherine's voice and how their fingers had touched when she had lit the cigarette for him, that afternoon by the river pool. He saw her face as she surfaced from under the water, her hair wet and her eyes sparkling. 'Why don't you come in?' The laughter in her voice. 'You must open your eyes underneath and see the colours. I'm going to try and paint them. I learnt to swim here in this pool with Maria. We've been right down this river to the cutting.'

He started arranging the stones on the grave. There should be something to make it different from the holes they dug and covered when they had to slaughter sick cattle. And if no human saw it, then God would see it from up there. He formed the stones into a cross. It was going to be all right. Time would pass and he would go to Hebron. He would take Catherine a gift, a painting of underneath the water in the pool – of what it looked like when he dived in and opened his eyes.

He sat for a while longer on the ledge whittling at a piece of wood with his knife, then he made his way back through the rocks.

*

Maria found Catherine at the pool wading knee high in the cold water. She had taken off her skirt and was bent over, feeling in the mud and reeds along the edge for something. She pulled up a rock, washed the mud off, and held it up to the light, then dropped it back in the water and started again. After a while she stopped, turned around, and saw Maria. 'How long have you been there?' she asked her.

'I didn't want to disturb you. What are you looking for?'

'I don't know.'

'What is it? You thought it was an accident, you wanted to think that but now you don't know anymore? Why don't I help you?'

'No. I don't need help. I just need some time.' Catherine had stepped out of the water and was searching along under the bushes.

'I came to tell you that I'd made supper.'

'It doesn't make sense.' Catherine hadn't heard Maria. 'Where is she? Where did he bury her?'

'I made supper.' Maria tried again.

'I'll be up just now.'

'It's getting dark.'

'You go ahead. I'll be there in half an hour. I just need to think.' Catherine sat down with her head in her hands.

Maria didn't want to leave her there, but there was no choice. If she didn't leave, Catherine would shout at her. She had been shouting a lot since she had closed that door on Tom. Maria had tried to distract Catherine. But when she had told her, 'everything will be okay,' she had felt guilty because it was what her own mother had told her when the man she had loved had died and she had spent all those days on his grave. She had thrown stones at her mother and screamed at her to leave her alone. She could have crushed her mother's head at that moment.

Catherine came back from the river, having found nothing. Maria took her a cup of tea, but Catherine didn't drink it. She just sat and stared out at the gum trees, not seeing anything. 'Let's put some music on,' Maria suggested.

'I don't feel like music.' Catherine shivered.

'You can't sit there every night like that.'

'Why not?'

'It will get too cold soon.' That would normally have made Catherine laugh, but she didn't even smile. 'Music might be fun. We can dance.' Maria tried again. 'Tomorrow we can go driving up along to the waterfall. I can drive.'

Catherine asked Maria to fetch her cigarettes. Maria got herself a book to read at the same time but she couldn't concentrate. 'We could go on holiday.' She looked up.

'We don't have any money.' Catherine was tapping out a staccato, agitated rhythm with her fingers on the wall. 'I went out to the airfield today. His plane is gone.'

'He could have sold it.'

Catherine frowned at her. 'He wouldn't do that. He loves that plane. No, he came back to get it. He came back and he didn't come here.'

'He doesn't know what you'll do, now that you know the truth. He's frightened. You sent him away.'

'Don't defend him, Maria.'

'I'm not.' Maria paused. 'What would you do – if he came back?'

'I don't know.' Catherine got up and walked the length of the stoep. 'I don't know. I just miss him, that's all.' She crushed her cigarette out.

'I was looking for a rock in the pool. A rock with blood on it. Where is it?' Catherine lit another cigarette. 'Why doesn't he come back?'

'Shall I run you a bath?' Maria stood up.

'I don't want a bath,' Catherine snapped. Maria left her. There was nothing more she could say.

Twenty

Hendrik takes the painting from underneath the altar in the church where he has hidden it. He has been working on it for a week now. He stands it on the easel he has brought with him from home. Then he turns up the paraffin flame so that he can see what he's doing. There are small marks on the paint and he runs his finger over them. He likes to think that they are small fingerprints, but they might have been caused by mice running over the wet paint in the dark. He mixes his paints and starts to put the finishing touches to the canvas. He paints over the scratch marks, but leaves one. By the time Catherine gets to the church he will be finished. She is coming to the church to meet him; he wrote her a note and left it at Hebron.

He is happy with the painting. She looks beautiful. Her skin shimmers with silver in the water on the canvas. She isn't cold, even though she is naked on the canvas. She's smiling at him. She likes it underwater in the pool. Her hair spreads out around her face. It's a clear, silent underwater world with no pain, no trouble, just a quiet breath, in and out – the small bubbles rise from her lips. It is like the veld, sparkling after the rain has washed the dust away. He is finished now. He stands back and looks at the painting, then he scratches his name at the bottom.

Catherine is nervous as she takes the path up to the church. *I have something for you* … he had written. He knew something. He was always watching at the pool, he had seen that night, he knew it was an accident, he would be able to tell her. He could have seen something. She had told Maria where she was going. Maria had warned her not to.

'He's in love with you,' she had said.

'That's nonsense,' Catherine had retorted. 'Sometimes your head is so full of nonsense.'

Hendrik is sitting on one of the pews. He gets up when Catherine comes in and comes forward towards her so that he can see her face. He has never felt so nervous and calm at the same time. She looks so lovely. She's wearing her yellow dress, the one she wore the first day she arrived when she stood outside the church.

'What is it?' She smiles at him and he can see that she's nervous. 'What do you want to tell me? Did you see something?' He wasn't expecting this. He had said he wanted to show her something. She must think … And now he could see why she looked nervous and excited, she thought … 'You haven't found anything?' Her voice is tense, she must have seen the disappointment on his face.

He shakes his head. 'No. I …'

'Then why did you ask me to come here?' She is angry now.

It is going wrong. It was too soon. He should have waited.

'You said you wanted to show me something.'

'Yes.'

He hesitates, but he can't think of anything that won't sound ridiculous. He has to show her the painting. There is no other explanation, and she is waiting. He moves slowly, as though his feet are in sinking sand, to fetch the paraffin lamp off the altar. She has seen the easel now, in the shadows. She is walking towards it.

He holds the lamp up so that she can see, but he looks out of the window, not at her. He doesn't want to see her face when she sees it. The moonlight is playing in the trees. He wants to be outside.

'This painting isn't of me.' She is speaking. He can't look at her. He concentrates on the branches, he thinks they are moving gently. He is trying not to panic. 'I didn't give you permission to paint this.' Her voice is cold. 'Look at me.'

But he can't.

'This isn't me. You haven't seen me …' He hears something break in her voice and his eyes flicker to her face. 'You can't come here. This church is on my land. I don't want you here ever again. Do you understand? This is not your place.' She stands there in front of him and he can't look at her. There is nothing he can say.

Catherine turns and runs out of the church.

'If you run fast enough can you run out of your body?'

'Why would you want to do that?'

'What if you want to disappear?'

'You mean die?'

'No.'

'I don't understand.'

'What if you want to just disappear. Into the rocks and the water and the sky and the earth – into laughter?'

'Why?'

'Then you can be here always. You don't have to leave.'

This is my pool, my church, my land.

★

Hendrik arrives at home but he doesn't remember how he got there. His mother has set a place for him at the table. The food is getting cold. They have been waiting for him. 'You look pale. What's wrong?' she asks him. He shakes his head. He feels like he is not himself, that he is acting in a play as he sits and slices the meat on his plate. 'Hendrik, you're ill.'

'No.'

'You fuss too much.' His father helps himself to more potatoes.

'I'm his Ma.'

'If you go on like that he'll leave us.'

'You wouldn't do that. Hendrik?'

He can't eat anymore. He gets up and excuses himself. 'I'm just tired.'

He walks out of the house down to the stables. It doesn't matter if they see him leaving, there is no need to hide. He finds a can of petrol and a rope, there are matches in his pocket.

As he walks across the veld he feels the wind on his face. A strange peace fills his heart. His senses have become so fine, like a needle in the grooves of one of those records at Hebron, releasing the sound and the joy. It is beautiful – the veld in the evening light, the sounds of the night creatures stirring.

At the koppie he climbs up one of the boulders and finds a place to lie. It doesn't matter what the time is. He doesn't have to get back for anything.

Out here in the dark above him there is a thin moon rising and in the sea of darkness the lights of the farms and kraals in the veld are like the stars above his head. Is he upside down? Which is heaven, which is earth?

There is no hurry. He can hear the singing and he imagines her standing in front of the painting. Her thin legs are like twigs under her dress with the peacocks embroidered around the hem and her hair is electric in the candlelight. She is laughing as she slides her bracelets up and down her arm.

*

Maria sees the glow from the church as she is walking back across the veld from her mother's place. She doesn't run because at first she thinks it is a light and she knows that the Afrikaans boy goes up there at night. Catherine is in her thoughts as she walks. The bucket with samp and beans from her mother bounces against her legs. When they are sitting together at Hebron she will tell Catherine of her plan for them to make money. She will heat the samp and beans for their supper. There is another thought that tries to make her listen to it, a thought about what she has told and what she has kept secret, but she pushes it back into the corners of her head, hoping it will lose itself there.

When she breathes in the night air she can smell the smoke now. She has reached the base of the koppie and, looking up, she sees that the smoke is coming from the church. There is a fire.

She pulls the blanket around her and starts to run. When she reaches the church her chest is heaving. If there was time she would go down to the river pool and soak her blanket in the water but there isn't. Instead she shouts out in the dark in case someone is walking home across the veld and will hear her and help. A pall of smoke hits her as she pushes the door open.

After it is over she can't remember what she saw first: the painting on fire, or Hendrik.

She covers her mouth and nose with the blanket, runs to the front of the church and pulls the altar table over and climbs on top so that she can reach Hendrik. He is so heavy to lift. He is hanging from the central beam but he is alive, she knows he is. She has seen dead bodies before. And then Gabriel is in the doorway, somehow he heard her call and he is beside her untying the rope and they lift Hendrik down and take him outside.

Maria breathes air into his lungs, she has read how to do this in the book on first aid, and soon he splutters and is breathing. She sits with his head in her lap and sends Gabriel to Hebron to tell Catherine. 'Tell her to bring the car to the store, then come back up to help carry him down. We need to go to the hospital.' She tells him to hurry. 'Go,' she snaps at him, 'what are you waiting for?'

The boy's eyes are opening. She doesn't know if he can hear her. She strokes his head and whispers to him. 'Why did you do such a stupid thing? There was no need. You should tell her the truth.'

On the way to hospital Maria sits with him in the back as Catherine drives. She has never driven so fast. Maria is not allowed into the white part of the hospital. She waits while a nurse fetches a stretcher. Catherine goes inside to give the staff his details so that they can call his parents. There is nothing more they can do.

Twenty-one

I think I must write this letter to you. There are things you should know that I could not tell you.

Hendrik crumpled the paper up and took another sheet from the pad. He was running out of paper. The red mark on his neck was beginning to fade now, but he hadn't been back to school since the hospital. His mother was distraught; she blamed Catherine and the native girl. He had escaped the house and gone to sit in the stables up on top of a hay bale. All he wanted was some peace to write this letter. Outside the stable his father started up the tractor. He was going to the railway siding to fetch mealie meal. There was a story that his mother and father were telling their friends and the teachers at school – it was that someone tried to strangle Hendrik in the native church, and everyone believed them because it was a native church and it confirmed all the rumours they would like to believe. His mother couldn't forgive Catherine King for what she had done to her son. She told Nettie the truth, she was the only one, and Nettie told her to be thankful the native girl found him in time and that they took him to the hospital, but his mother just shook her head. She wouldn't hear it.

I came up to the church. I go there often. I like to be there.

Hendrik stared out of the door of the stables. He could see his horse down in the camp but he hadn't gone riding for weeks. It hadn't rained either for weeks. Winter was on its way; the colours were changing in the veld.

Most times I go to the church at night, in the dark. But that day I went in the afternoon.

That day, the day Isobel died, his father had sent him to get the horses in. There was going to be a storm and they were running wild in the field, galloping up and down – as though the electricity in the air affected them. It had taken him a long time to even get near them so that he could put a rope around their necks and quieten them down, to take them inside. Slowly they let him get closer and he had put his hand on his horse's neck and breathed into her skin. He loved the smell of her.

'I'm going to tell Catherine about the children in the church,' he had told his horse. 'I'm going to paint her something too. She'll know that we're meant to be together. Mr Fyncham can't see the children – only me. There are two girls. I can hear them. I heard them long before I met her. I knew who she was.'

His mother was standing outside waiting for him when he came up to the house from the stables. She asked him to get the paraffin from the shed.

When I left the house I thought it will storm soon.

He had run most of the way to the church. He had wanted to go swimming in the pool. He had wanted to be in the water when the lightning struck on the koppies. He was happy.

It was still light when I reached the church. I started to paint. I wanted to finish the painting of you and then go for a swim.

In the church he had felt them behind him. They were watching. He could feel their breath.

'What is it?' they whispered. He could feel them moving around the painting.

'Maybe it's upside down.'

'Maybe you're upside down.'

'Maybe the church is upside down.'

They laughed.

He had heard the rumbling of thunder, but it was still far away. The sun was dropping in the sky when he went outside the church. The whole veld was bathed in a luminous light. All the colours were merged into an electric green and gold.

I went down between the trees. I was going to jump off the ledge into the pool. Like you do.

But he had stopped when the ledge came into view because someone was standing on the rocks overlooking the pool.

Someone had got there before me. It was Mrs Fyncham.

She had been standing on the rock with her back to him staring down into the pool and he had known then that something was wrong. She was wearing a dress; she wasn't in a bathing suit to go swimming. He had thought that perhaps she was watching someone in the pool.

I never drew her. The sketch in my sketchbook was of you. I was embarrassed to tell you because of what you would think of me. I didn't think Mrs Fyncham was going to jump.

But then she had moved forward on the ledge and closed her eyes, swaying slightly, and he had known what she was going to do. She was trying to be brave enough to jump. He had done the same thing. He had heard Catherine's voice. 'Come on, jump.

Jump out, otherwise you'll slip. You have to jump out. You have to not think. Don't think.'

She stood there for a long time. And then he heard Tom call her name.

I should have told her to jump out. I should have stopped her. I heard Mr Fyncham calling her.

Catherine sat down. She didn't want to read on because she knew what was going to happen.

'Look at me, Dad.'

'Come on Katie. Don't be a chicken. Jump.'

'I can't.'

'Of course you can.'

'Jump out.'

'One, two ...'

She's in the water.

He's holding her in his arms, swinging her high.

'You're a brave girl. I've got a brave daughter.'

'I'm not a chicken, am I?'

'No, you're not a chicken.'

'Maria thinks there are chickens in the sky. She's crazy isn't she?'

Catherine went on reading. She couldn't stop.

As she stepped forward to jump, she looked up towards the tin church as if she heard something, as if someone has called her name and she said 'yes'. But when I turned around I couldn't see anyone, or hear anything. If she had not turned then she would not have slipped. But she fell and her head smashed against the rock.

I was going to run down but Mr Fyncham was there. He tried to breathe air into her lungs but she must have been dead already. He went back down the path, I think he was going to get help but I couldn't be sure.

I didn't want you to see Mrs Fyncham in your pool. I thought you would leave the farm. I was scared you would leave. I hope you understand why I had to bury her. You couldn't know. You couldn't leave – you belong here.

He had written at the bottom in small print.

I love you
Hendrik.

Catherine folded the letter up. Maria had come out with the bowl of potatoes she was peeling. She sat on the step, waiting for Catherine to say something. 'Did you know what happened that evening? Did you tell Hendrik to write this letter to me?' Catherine knew the answer. She just wanted Maria to say it. 'Why? Why didn't you tell me? What were you thinking?'

Maria put the bowl down on the floor and the knife beside it. She wiped her hands on her skirt and looked down to where Gabriel was working in the vegetable garden. 'I don't know. I thought it could be as it was.'

'It can't. You know that. I've tried. I just can't.' Maria got up and went through to the kitchen. 'Where are you going?' Catherine called after her.

But she didn't answer. She was trying to find a ripe prickly pear in amongst the ones she had picked in the garden to put in the cardboard box for Catherine. It was a picnic.

'For your journey,' she told Catherine as she handed her the box, 'I packed some food so you wouldn't be hungry.'

Maria watched Catherine drive away and then she got her blanket and took it out under the peach tree where she sat for a long time staring out down the road. She felt like that girl, Eustacia, in the book – watching through her telescope in the dark.

Twenty-two

It is early evening when Catherine parks the car under the trees in the square in LM. She is hot and thirsty and walks across the square to where a man is selling cold drinks. The smell of the sea is strong from here. People are out walking on the streets after the heat of the day. She finds a bench and sits down to drink her Coca-Cola. Couples stroll hand in hand. A priest passes her on his way to the church. A group of young schoolgirls giggle as they try and eat their ice-lollies before they melt and drip onto their white shirts.

There is music playing from a bar across the road and a group of black women are standing teasing a man. They laugh. He strikes a match against his shoe and lights his cigarette with it – this makes them laugh and tease him more.

People look at her as they walk past. She looks dishevelled. Her hair is wild from driving with the window wide open and her face is grimy with dust. She is going to find Tom. They can go somewhere, they don't have to go back to the farm, not immediately. Perhaps they can stay at the coast for a while.

The drink is cold and very fizzy; she can feel the bubbles in her nose. A car parks in an empty bay on the opposite side of the street and a woman gets out. She is carrying a gift, a fruit basket wrapped in cellophane; she has put on her best dress and shoes. Another car parks behind hers and a family get out. They too are carrying a gift.

Across the square the clock strikes six o'clock. Catherine thinks they must be going to the church but they start to walk in the opposite direction. They disappear behind some trees and she gets up and walks across the road to see where they are going.

The hospital is an old colonial building with a flight of stairs leading up to a vast wooden door; it must be visiting hour because there is a long line of people.

There is a red cross painted above the door and the words written in black paint. 'Hospital de Santa Maria.'

She stands there watching them going in. Such a small thing – a cross drawn on the ground. A mistake.

Mr King is at Santa Maria?

Sim, Santa Maria.

Then she gets up and crosses the street. There is a crowd of people at the hospital reception and she has to wait.

'Mr King.' She has to spell it out. She knows she's crazy asking this.

The receptionist looks through her records.

'No. No Mr King. Sorry.'

'Are you sure?'

The woman turns around and calls to her colleague.

'One minute.'

She waits. The colleague reappears with one of the nurses. They talk in Portuguese. Catherine can't understand.

The nurse smiles. 'There was Mr King here.' She speaks slowly and in broken English. 'I am sorry, he died.'

'When did he die?'

The nurse looks through a register.

'Nine months ago. It was in the winter.'

Catherine thinks of the letter, of the night she saw him standing on the edge of the river. It had happened then, when she was in England. He had died and Isobel and Tom had come to the farm.

'Are you a friend?' the nurse asks and Catherine realises she has been standing there for five minutes.

'I'm his daughter.'

'Katie?'

She nods.

'He talk about you too much. He say I make him think of you, my face.' She looks down, embarrassed now. They stand awkwardly. Catherine doesn't know what to say. 'He's bury in the church, across the square. No …' the nurse smiles, remembering something. 'No buried. He didn't want to be in coffin. He say sometime people put you in when you no really dead. I tell him is not true.'

'Across the square?'

'Yes, but is mass now. You go in morning. The man he will tell you where your father's ashes are in the church. Your father wanted to see you again. You were his special one.'

Catherine starts to walk towards the door, but the nurse calls after her and she turns back.

'Your father's wife, she was brought in here.'

'When?'

'About month ago. It was her heart.'

'She's dead?'

The nurse nods.

'Yes. Her daughter die in an accident – I think this news too much for her mother. Her heart stopped.'

'Who brought her in?'

'Daughter's husband. She have no one else.'

Catherine walks back out into the dusk and starts to walk down the streets. She should really find somewhere to sleep because she is exhausted now, but she doesn't want to be inside.

A little girl is chasing a boy down the street. He has stolen something of hers and she is running shouting after him. Catherine follows her. The streets have got narrower. The girl turns a corner. There is a small square and pepper trees. A slab for gutting fish. Catherine knows where she is now.

The boy turns around and pulls a face at the girl who is out of breath, bent over with her hands on her knees. She stands up and shouts and starts to chase him again.

The street is cobbled. It leads down to the water. Fishermen are tying a boat up to a small jetty and taking the fish out of the boat. She doesn't know if she can find her way back now. But it doesn't matter. She takes off her sandals. The air is warm and full of all those different smells.

The walls of the fortress are lit by the moon that is full and hanging like a huge ball over the bay. It's high tide and the water covers the bottom steps of the crumbling building. And there is the palm tree from the postcard, from her dream, where it should be in the central square. It's warm and she feels like swimming.

She climbs up the steps and walks along. The girl has caught up with the boy. They are walking along one of the high walls above her. Catherine sees that there is a small beach on the other side of the fortress. She finds her way down. Nobody will notice if she takes off her clothes and goes for a swim.

There is phosphorescence on the water and it sparkles on her skin as she swims out. She looks across the bay where Tom's house is all lit up in the dark.

Twenty-three

'She's gone. She wants to find him.'

'It's the best thing really – that she's left the farm. She's caused enough trouble.'

'She'll be back though.'

'Yes, when she realises that he'll never leave his wife.'

'He'll sell the farm. The wife won't want to come back here.'

'They never belonged.'

Nettie spreads out the colour samples on the table. She is painting her house and can't decide on the pale pink or pale yellow. 'It depends on the light of course – in the room. The man in the shop said that if there's pink in the room it will pick up on it and make a nice glow.'

'You've got those embroidered cushions from the kerkbasaar.' Hendrik's mother looks at her own sitting room. 'Maybe I should paint in here. It's so dark. What do you think?' Nettie looks around the room.

'Yes it could do with something bright.'

'I've been thinking of getting rid of the furniture.'

'What, do you mean all of it?'

'No – these heavy chairs. They're so gloomy. At least that's what Hendrik says, and I agree with him. I hadn't noticed how old and frayed they were getting.'

'How is Hendrik?'

'He's recovering.'

They are silent.

'Has he been back up to the church?'

'No,' his mother says quickly. 'Do you know I wish the whole place had burnt down. I can't help it. It's not a church, you know. Not really. A church is where people gather to worship God. Churches are built to the glory of God.' But she didn't say it with great conviction. 'Nettie?'

'What is it?' Nettie looks up from the paint samples.

'When was the last time you went down to the river?'

'Oh, goodness.'

'Let's go to the river. Let's take a picnic. Hendrik built a raft down there with Dirk, you know. We could …' Nettie starts to laugh. 'Don't laugh. I've been all the way down to the cutting. When we were first married we had a canoe. I rowed all the way down. Marius just lay there and watched me. He said …' She looks out of the window. 'He said, "you've got the most beautiful smile," that's what he said.'

Hendrik watches them setting off across the veld with their baskets and their hats. Nettie has borrowed one from his father that is slightly too small for her head, and it perches on top. 'If we aren't back by six come and look for us, Hendrik,' his mother laughs. 'We're going to row down the river. I'm going to show Nettie. Do you remember when we all went down?'

He feels light watching them laughing together like that as they walk away from him. He feels a joy creeping into his heart for another reason too. Catherine has come back. Although he hasn't seen her, he has seen her car in town.

It is six o'clock and his mother and Nettie haven't come back, but he tells himself that it is likely that they have gone to Nettie's house for tea. He will wander down to the river to look anyway. It's a beautiful afternoon.

He is at the foot of the koppies when he hears the aeroplane and looks up. It is circling the church and he stands watching as it climbs and falls and turns.

*

Maria stands and squints up into the sky at the giant insect. She is standing in the graveyard outside the church waiting for Catherine to throw the ashes. She won't be able to see the ashes falling but she will imagine them floating down in the blue and she will shout something into the sky, she isn't sure what though.

From the aeroplane, Catherine can see Maria standing and waving.

'Turn the plane,' she shouts at Tom. She has been shouting at him all the way back from the coast. But he is the only person who can take her up in the air where she wants to be. She has brought her father's ashes back.

Maria had told her a story of ashes. If you threw them in the wrong wind, they could blow back onto you. Someone had got the ashes of her third cousin once removed in her mouth. It was horrible, horrible. They had laughed.

And then she throws her father's ashes and watches as they are taken by the wind. They will come down to rest, on the rocks and trees and in the river. Perhaps some will even fall on the roof of the church. He will be there forever.

Hendrik watches as the plane turns one last time and then flies off down over the krantz. He becomes aware of someone standing behind him. She must have come up quietly – someone who is used to walking silently across the veld. He can feel her a few feet behind him.

'I wish I could fly,' she says. 'Sometimes I think I can.' He turns around. 'What's in your bag?' she asks him.

'Nothing.'

'Can I have a look?'

He takes out the sketchbook. He doesn't care anymore who sees his sketches. He is going to leave them in the church. He hands it to her.

Elise squats down on the ground and opens the book carefully.

When she sees the children in the church she looks up at him and smiles.

Epilogue: 1990

'There you are.' Maria finds Catherine lying by the river pool. She is wrapped in a blanket and Maria takes her hands. They are icy cold. She rubs them to warm them up. 'You shouldn't be doing this. You're freezing. And we're too old. It's not safe.'

'I'm not too old. And safe – what is safe?' Catherine sits up. 'I was on my way to the church. There was a light on.'

'I know, I saw it from the house.'

'Remember our wish? Do you remember when we buried Tom at the church, how we heard the singing? How difficult it was when he first came back here. How we used to fight?'

'You – always making him prove himself. All the time. You drove him mad.' Maria laughs.

'But then it was okay.'

'Yes.'

'I still miss him.'

Catherine leans against Maria as she stands up. Her legs are stiff.

'I won't let you go alone.' Maria looks up at the trees above the pool. The shadows look like figures dancing between the tree trunks in the moonlight.

Catherine leads the way slowly up the path. They have to stop to rest half way up, then again near the top. 'We used to laugh at the gogos walking so slowly up this hill.' Catherine's chest feels raw. 'I don't feel old – I feel that I could still run up here, and still jump off the ledge into the pool.'

'And kill yourself?'

'We thought the light in the church was a miracle.' They are standing in the doorway of the church now looking in at the paraffin lamp burning on the altar.

'You never told me what it was you saw in there.' Maria looks at Catherine, but Catherine's not going to tell her, even now. It will always be a secret. Sometimes you need a secret. 'You go in – I'll be out here.' Maria turns to go.

The church is empty. Hendrik hasn't waited then. The painting is hanging on the wall where her picture used to be, the one that burnt in the fire. But here is something in its place. Something beautiful.

Catherine goes to fetch the paraffin lamp from the altar and holds it up in front of the painting.

Hendrik has painted the church half in shadow, half in light, and two girls standing in front of the altar. They have on their summer dresses, one orange, one pale yellow. They look luminous as if they are lit up from the inside. Their hair is wild and the air is electric around them. She can hear them laughing.

You'll never catch us. Nobody will. We'll always be separate.

Catherine leaves the church and finds Maria standing in the middle of the graveyard staring at a cleared patch of ground in front of her. 'This is what the Afrikaans boy was doing up here.' Maria turns to her. She still calls Hendrik a boy.

He has been at the edge of their lives all these years – helping them: when the police had come; when Catherine was struggling on the farm to make money and pay the bills; when a group of farmers had stood in the driveway at Hebron with guns, wanting to know why Maria lived with Catherine in the house, why she was a kaffir-lover. Hendrik had stood there beside her until they had left.

Catherine bends down to look at what Hendrik has written with small white stones on the earth. She runs her fingers over the letters.

Isobel.

'He moved her bones.' She looks up at Maria. 'But why did he dig them up now?' Maria smooths the earth around the stones. 'It was you, Maria, wasn't it? You dug the bones up. Why?'

'I wanted her to be buried here, properly, before I die.'

'You're not going to die.'

Maria is silent.

'Have you seen it?' Catherine shakes Maria's shoulder.

'It was hard work digging with that spade. Then it started to rain. I didn't have time. And when I came back after the girl had found her bones, he had moved them.'

'It's better like this.' Catherine stands up.

'It's good. They weren't in a good place.' Maria shakes her head. 'She was lonely there on that ledge.' Catherine spreads Maria's blanket next to the grave and sits down.

'I'm so tired,' she says. 'Let's rest here a while before we go back.' They lie down next to each other for warmth and look up at the night sky.

'What would those women say if they saw me now? Out here in the dark in a graveyard with the mad black kitchen girl.'

'Can you hear that?' Maria turns to Catherine.

'You hear something?'

'Just the river.'

*

The sun is up and the girl who found the bones is climbing up the path to the church. She has come to look at the place where she found the bones once more. Just to make sure of what she really saw that day. She scrambles through the opening in the rocks and squats down on the ground. The earth has been smoothed over and she is wondering if she really saw anything on this ledge above the valley when she hears the laughter.

Two girls are running past the rocks and down the hill from the church. The little black girl is chasing – the white girl is not far ahead. Their feet are bare and their dresses are dirty from playing.

Suddenly they stop – they have heard something. Someone is calling them and they look back up at the church. Another girl is standing in the doorway waving.

'Wait for me,' she calls and starts to run down the hill after them. Her black hair streams behind her in the wind.

Acknowledgements

For Katrina Themba and the remarkable women in my family who lived in this place, whose stories I grew up on, and whose paintings surrounded me: Ruth Everard Haden, Rosamund Everard Steenkamp, Bertha Everard King and Edith King. They, together with my father Bryan Everard Haden, were the inspiration for this story.

I would especially like to thank Dorothy Dyer for her support and guidance in editing the manuscript. I would also like to thank Frances Liardet, Pippa Davies, Mary Mount, Angela Briggs, Kathy Sutton and Irna du Toit for their advice, support and encouragement. Thank you Andrea – for your 'attic' and your cooking! I am also indebted to the Baird Foundation for their financial support during my MA in Creative Writing at UCT and to my supervisor Geoffrey Haresnape.